PLAYING THE NEUTRAL ZONE

S.L. STERLING

PLAYING THE NEUTRAL ZONE

by

S.L. Sterling

©2025

1

Playing the Neutral Zone

Copyright © 2025 by S.L. Sterling

ISBN: 978-1-998649-00-6

Paperback ISBN: 978-1-989566-94-7

Harcover ISBN: 978-1-989566-95-4

Editor: Brandi Aquino, Editing Done Write

Cover Design: Thunderstruck Cover Design

Chapter One

Scarlett - Seven Years Ago

I LAY ON THE LOUNGE, staring up at the sky. I'd always loved watching the clouds drift overhead as the sun beat down on me, and now was no different. I could hear the traffic of New York city in the distance, which I found oddly relaxing.

I inhaled deeply, trying to focus on the moment and not think about the fact that soon I'd be back at school for my last semester of college. Nerves and anxiety would build, and all the fun of this past summer would be behind me, but for now, I needed to remind myself to just enjoy the present moment.

I spent most of my summer travelling with my

parents and my brother Scott. Probably the last family vacation we'd take, since Scottie was now engaged to be married to his high school sweetheart, Monica. I'd soon be permanently living in New York, especially once I graduated from school in six months, as that was where all the jobs were.

Levi was my brother's best friend. He was also the man I'd planned to spend the rest of my life with when I was only thirteen, and it still held true today—for me anyway. Levi wouldn't date me because he'd made some silly promise to my brother that he wouldn't lay a finger on me until I graduated school. He valued his friendship with my brother, but he'd also told him once graduation day came, I was fair game, and that there would be no more bro code shit.

Over the years we'd flirt, we'd kiss, and we'd dance around one another, even while we both dated other people. Most of the time I focused my time trying to get his attention, but no matter what I did, the man wouldn't crack. That was okay though, because when it came down to it, we both knew we were the one for each other.

Levi had just signed a five-year contract with the New York Predators, and he'd just purchased a new condo in one of the newest high-rises in the Upper East Side this spring. I could still remember the day he called to tell me and Scottie the news, he sounded like a little kid at Christmas, but once he got me on the phone alone, that's when things changed. His voice went from that giddy child's voice to that deep, sexy voice I loved.

"Now we can proceed as planned. Once you're done with school, we'll find you a job close to the condo, and you can just move in."

"Here you go, my sun goddess." Levi said, interrupting my thoughts.

I looked over and shaded my eyes from the sun to see him standing there shirtless, holding out a glass of iced tea. The moment I returned, I came out here so I could spend my last week of summer vacation with Levi as I had done every summer. I smiled and sat up and took the glass from him while he straddled the lounger I was lying on and sat down behind me.

"Thank you." I softly smiled and took a sip of the perfectly sweetened iced tea.

When I sat back, Levi wrapped his arms around my waist and placed a kiss on the side of my neck.

I closed my eyes and relished the warmth of his touch. I loved the way it felt to be in his arms and could only imagine how much better it would feel once things were out in the open neutral I was finally his.

I'd just placed my glass down on the table when he started kissing my neck. Only when his lips hit the spot just below my ear, I couldn't help but laugh.

"God, I love how ticklish you are," he whispered, his breath causing me to laugh more as he kissed that spot again.

I shifted on the seat and turned, moving to meet his lips, but he placed his forefinger on them, stopping me.

"You know we can't do anything yet. I made a promise."

I rolled my eyes. How I hated that stupid promise he'd made to my brother.

"You're seriously going to wait?" I questioned, my voice cracking. "It's six more months."

"I am. I made a promise to your brother. What kind of friend would I be if I went back on my word?" He leaned back against the chair, looking at me with his gorgeous baby blues.

"This is so stupid. Levi, you're a grown man, and I'm a grown woman. We are both capable of making our own decisions."

"You don't need to remind me," he said, his eyes skimming down my bikini-clad body. "I'll be just as happy to rip this off you when the time comes as you'll be to have it ripped off." He smiled, running his finger under the shoulder strap of my bathing suit.

He didn't know just how happy I'd be to have that happen. I'd only been dreaming of it for what felt like forever, wondering what it would be like to feel the weight of him on top of me.

"It's six more months, Levi. I don't think that's going to make a difference. Let's just start seeing one another now. Scottie doesn't need to know. We're all the way out here. He's all the way back home. Plus, Monica has him consumed with wedding plans."

Levi met my eyes, a small smile on his lips, but then shook his head. "I'll know."

"You're turning me down?" I questioned.

"Not turning you down. I'm keeping my word to someone who means a lot to me. Plus, it's six months. We've waited this long. Another six months won't kill us."

"Easy for you to say."

"What is that supposed to mean?" he asked, placing his finger under my chin and lifting my head so I could look at him.

"It means I'm dying here, Levi. I'm seriously dying. I want to be with you."

"And you will be."

I crossed my arms and let out a sigh. "Okay, well, what happens if I meet someone this year, and he sweeps me right off my feet? Then, because of that, we never have the chance to be together because I am head over heels in love with him."

"Not going to happen."

"How are you so sure? It could happen."

"Scarlett, let's be real. You only have eyes for me. I

know it, you know it. It's not like you haven't dated others. If we weren't meant to be, you'd have met someone by now and would have run away with him already. A few more months will hurt nothing." He winked, then placed a kiss on the top of my head and got up off the lounger. "What do you want on your pizza? Same as always?"

I lay back and watched as he walked across the patio, picking up his phone. My eyes washed over his body and travelled back up in time to meet his eyes as he turned around. I softly smiled. "You know me too well," I answered, taking another drink of my iced tea.

I CLOSED my eyes just as the credits rolled. I lay on the couch, Levi lay behind me, a blanket thrown across our legs, while his arms wrapped around me. He smells so good, I thought to myself as I took a deep breath.

"What did you want to watch now, or did you want to hit the hay?" he asked.

I rubbed my eyes. I didn't want to go to sleep because sleep meant that I'd have to move to the guest bedroom. Yep, he refused to even share a bed with me.

"Why don't we watch something scary?" I questioned.

"Something scary? Don't you remember the last time we watched something scary?"

I shook my head, knowing full well what had happened the last time. It was the night of my sixteenth birthday, and I'd been so frightened in the middle of the night I'd gotten up, rushed across the hall to our spare bedroom where I knew Levi was sleeping. I'd thrown open his bedroom door, fully prepared to crawl into bed with him like I'd done many times before, only to find him… God the memory flooded my body with heat. It had been the first time I'd ever seen a man naked.

My cheeks flooded with heat, and for the first time, I was thankful I wasn't facing him.

"That was different. I was only in my teens. God, I'm a grown woman now."

"I'll never forget the way your eyes washed over my body that night…the color of your cheeks…the shock on your face…" he muttered.

"Well, it's not every day a fifteen-year-old walks in on her older brother's best friend to find him…indisposed."

He let out a throaty chuckle, and then I felt him shift away from me for a moment, turning onto his back and pulling the covers off me a little.

"What are you doing?

"Covering myself," he said, adjusting the blanket over himself.

"Well, I'm cold. Probably had too much sun today," I said, reaching behind me and pulling the blanket back over my legs.

"Scarlett, stop fucking around," he said as he pulled the blanket back on top of him. "You don't want to know what I have under this blanket."

I shifted myself so I was now facing him and propped myself up on my elbow, a playful grin coming to my lips.

"Maybe I do…" I said, twirling my hair around my finger.

He looked into my eyes, his face serious as the heat built between us like it had frequently before. It was always this way between us. He'd test me, I'd test him. It was the way we worked. It was the way we'd always worked, but in the end, his promise to my brother always won.

As our eyes remained locked, I felt his hand grab mine and before I could pull it away, he'd placed it on his hardened cock, holding it there, and closed his eyes.

Shock travelled up my arm, and I swallowed hard as my body heated while my hand cupped his shaft through the blanket, through his jeans, my memory flashing back to that night all those years ago. I'd seen him. I'd barged into his room after that stupid scary movie they'd forced me to watch and seen his cock in his hand as he stroked himself while laying naked on the bed, covers off to the side.

It had only been a glimpse, and I jumped as he shouted and covered himself up, causing me to slam the door shut and leave his room. I'd never really realized how big he was until this moment.

My mouth was dry, and I could feel my heart beating in my ears as I watched him bite his lower lip, his eyes closed while his hand was still resting on top of mine, holding it hostage. I licked my lips, and without barely making any movement, I slowly leaned down and pressed my lips to his.

We'd kissed millions of times before, but the moment our lips touched this time, electricity flooded my body. Internally, I screamed. My hand tightened around him. I didn't want this to stop. I wanted all of him right now. My mind flooded with thoughts of him pushing me away, of him leaving, but then his one arm wrapped around me, while the other pulled me down, and he kissed me back.

All this time, all this flirting and banter, finally maybe it was over, and we could take the next step toward becoming one.

His tongue washed through my mouth, as his hand fisted my hair, then cupped my cheek. I moved my hand off his cock and placed it on his hip as he slid his body closer to mine, grinding himself against me. I swung my leg onto his hip, wanting to feel more of him as he continued grinding into me. I felt the warmth of his smooth skin as my fingers trailed along his back.

I couldn't breathe—not because I was nervous, but because I was afraid any type of movement would make this moment end. I wanted us to cross this imaginary line, because until now, the most he'd ever done was cuddle me during a movie, place tiny kisses on my neck when we were alone, and flirt with me until I was ready to drop because he'd made me so weak in the knees.

I felt his fingers playing with the buttons on my shirt, and one by one he slowly undid them all, slipping his large hand into my shirt and gripping my side. He kissed me deeper, and when his thumb grazed the side of my breast, I let out a soft moan.

Just as I ran my fingers through his thick, dark hair, he broke the kiss and looked down at me, his hair disheveled.

He studied me, looking deep into my eyes. "We—"

I placed my fingers on his lips. "Don't say it," I whispered, my throat straining from the flood of emotions I was feeling. "Please…don't say it."

He looked down at me for what felt like forever, then he slowly lowered his head and took my lips with his, consuming my mouth. When he pulled his lips from mine and looked down at me again, I thought for sure he was going to say it, but he got up, shut the TV off, held out his hand for me to take, and led me down the hall.

I felt as if I were floating on a bed of clouds as I followed him, my hand in his. He met my eyes, softly smiled, and then stopped right outside the spare bedroom, pushed me up against the wall. He pressed himself against me, took my mouth with his, his tongue washing through my mouth as his hands explored me. Then he broke the kiss, pulled away and stepped back.

"I've wanted you for so long, Scarlett. I promised myself I'd never lay a finger on you until you're done school…and as fucking tempting as you are, I'm hell bent on keeping that promise."

I stood there, my body on fire as I watched his eyes wash over me while he slowly backed away.

"That's why I'm saying good night, Scarlett, and I'm going to ask that you don't come into my room tonight, because I don't think I have the strength to hold back much longer."

Six Months Later

"CONGRATULATIONS, SCARLETT."

I could feel my cheeks heat as Scottie and Levi stood there holding a small graduation cake in Levi's living room.

It just so happened that Levi had a couple days off from games and had invited me and Scottie to stay before we took off home to see Mom and Dad.

"I should also announce this isn't the only celebration," Levi added, slipping a knife through the cake.

"Oh, what else are we celebrating?" Scottie questioned.

"Well, I'll let Scarlett tell you," Levi added, popping a piece of cake on a plate for each of us.

Scottie looked over at me, a smile on his face as he waited for me to tell him.

"Now don't get too excited, but I got a job with *Ice Insiders*. I did a co-op for them this past semester, and while it's only a temp position for now, it has good promise to become something more once I prove myself."

"That's outstanding, Scarlett. So, you'll be staying in the city then?"

I glanced over at Levi. We'd kept our relationship on the quiet side for the past month, and a couple of weeks ago, with the news of the new position, just as planned, we were moving in together. I had no idea how Scottie was going to take this news. I still needed to tell Mom and Dad. I was probably crazy for telling Scottie first.

"I will be." I swallowed hard, still trying to gage his reaction.

"Well, I'd ask Levi to check in on you, but with his schedule, he's barely in the city."

"Don't be silly. You don't even need to ask. I'll keep an eye on her," Levi added, passing each of us a piece of cake.

"How are you going to do that? Like I said, you're barely here. I think I counted two weeks out of the past eleven." Scottie chuckled.

Levi and I looked at one another.

"Well, I've asked Scarlett to move in here. It will be perfect. Honestly, someone will be here while I'm out of town, and since the building is secure, I know she'll be safe," Levi added.

Scottie thought about it for a moment as he shoved a forkful of cake in his mouth and then nodded. "Might be a good idea, Scar. I mean rent out here— well, I can't even imagine what it must cost."

I looked at Levi, my hands shaking with nerves as Scottie still rambled on about rent, bills, and how what I would earn in a temp position couldn't possibly cover everything. How I'd never be able to support myself on that type of wage.

"We're dating, bro," Levi announced, saving me from having to tell him.

Scottie's head lifted so quickly, I feared it might pop off.

"What?"

"The reason I've asked her to move in isn't the reasons you're talking about. We're dating. We thought we should tell you first. After all, I promised you I'd never lay a hand on her until she graduated, and I told you once she had all promises were off."

Scottie was quiet for a few moments as he looked from me to Levi.

"You were serious?"

"Yes, he's serious, Scottie." I nervously laughed and reached over, placing my hand on his, hoping he wasn't going to be too angry.

"Well, you know I'm going to have to give him the lecture, right?" my brother said, looking at me.

I rolled my eyes at him. I'd have thought Levi had already proved himself to Scottie through this entire ordeal.

"Only if you feel it's necessary, but I can assure you he will not hurt me."

"Not gonna hurt her, bro. That I promise," Levi said.

"What kind of big brother would I be if I didn't say it?" Scottie asked, looking over at me.

"A shitty one." I giggled.

Levi and Scottie laughed at the same time and then gave one another a congratulatory fist bump.

The next morning, I had my shower and made my way down to the kitchen wrapped in my bathrobe. Levi looked over at me, a smile on his face as I took a seat at the breakfast bar.

"It's going to be so nice to have you here," Levi said, sliding a plate of pancakes my way.

"I know, I can't wait. My lease is up at the end of the month, which gives me time to go home, see my mom and dad and get back to the city to pack to move at the end of the month. Which, good news, I've already arranged a moving truck."

"Babe, you should know the guys and I will move you."

"No way, I'm not having the guys from the hockey team help move me. I barely know any of them, and besides, what if you're at an away game?"

"Well, you best get to know them. They are my second family, and my schedule is right here for the entire season." Levi winked, tapping the schedule that was on the side of his fridge.

Levi had just started eating while I shoved the last

few bites of my pancakes into my mouth when someone knocked on the door.

"That better not be them," I said, jumping off the stool, alarmed that I was naked under this bathrobe.

Levi chuckled before leaning down to kiss me.

"Might be. You never know." He winked. "Go on, go get dressed," he said, slapping my ass as I turned away from him, causing me to let out a giggle.

Once down the hall and in his bedroom, I took my time getting dressed, washing my face, and then I ran a brush through my hair and put it up in a high ponytail. I shoved my things into my bag and then made my way down the hall. I was just about in the kitchen when I heard voices. I stopped and listened. Was that a woman's voice I heard?

I stood still, listening. It *was* a woman's voice. At first, she was calm, but soon their voices started getting elevated, but I still couldn't make out their conversation as the exchange between them continued. Then things got quiet, and I heard Levi clear his throat and beg the person to wait.

A funny feeling settled in the pit of my stomach. I'd never heard Levi sound panicked before. He continued asking the person to wait, to give him a chance to figure out exactly what this was, and then the door slammed shut and the apartment was quiet.

I stood there for a moment. I wanted to give Levi a

few minutes to himself. I felt that whatever had just gone on wasn't really any of my business, but at the same time I wanted to know what had happened. I was about to turn and head back down the hall when I heard what sounded like a baby crying.

For a moment I froze, my stomach threatening to release the contents of the breakfast I'd just eaten. I tiptoed down the rest of the hallway and rounded the corner, stepping into the kitchen...and stopped dead in my tracks at the scene in front of me.

There, by the door, surrounded by a pile of bags at his feet, stood Levi.

And in his arms was a baby.

Chapter Two

Levi – Six Years Later

The sun shone through the floor-to-ceiling windows of my condo's living room. I took a sip of my coffee, quickly checking the time on my phone. It was five thirty; I had to be at the arena in an hour, which meant if we didn't get a move on, I'd be late for practice for the second time in the past week.

"Come on, Mia, get your things. We're going to be late," I called.

I scrolled through the email Lucas sent me from Pamela, our head of PR, as I took another mouthful of coffee, and then shoved the last of my hard-boiled egg into my mouth. Tonight, after the game, we were going to be interviewed by Scarlett Green, or I should say the team.

I'd been in a state of shock ever since the night of the barbeque when Lucas asked the guys if they'd heard of her. I knew I'd probably let it slip when my head shot up, but I was certain I'd done a good job of recovery. While I still kept in touch with her brother Scott on a weekly basis, he'd done a good job of not mentioning her to me ever again, just like I'd asked.

"Mia, let's go," I called again, annoyance in my voice.

I was just about to shove my phone in my pocket when it vibrated. I looked at the screen to see new messages from the guys.

Lucas: You dicks ready for tonight's interview with Ice Insiders....

Knox: Sure am, Lorelai has been grilling me with potential questions asked at other interviews. I should be golden.

Lucas: Why are you this way?

Knox: What? Prepared? Because I don't want to look like an idiot on camera...

Clay: You don't need to worry, you always look like an idiot.

Dylan: Whoa, those are some big words coming from a guy who's probably lying in bed with his sister right now.

Clay: Nope, in the car getting coffee. She's home laying in post coital bliss and those were her words, by the way.

Knox: I need to bleach my eyes now and you must need your teeth rearranged, again.

Dylan: Okay, this had better end before we get to practice. Can't have you two all bloody and bruised for pictures afterward. We'll talk more at practice, but we'd better be on game tonight.

Colton: Don't worry Dylan, Levi and I will help hold them back from one another should need be.

Levi: Speak for yourself...I'm not on the interview list for tonight

I tapped the edge of my phone and shut my screen off before shoving it into my pocket. I didn't want to face questions from the guys about why I wouldn't be there. The moment I heard that Scarlett was the one interviewing, I'd set up a private meeting with Pamela and requested I be excluded from tonight's interview.

I had my reasons for the request, which I was told would be better if I disclosed, but I kept them private. Pamela didn't need to know about my past, or about the fact that Scarlett had been the first and last person to break my heart into a million pieces, with zero chance of putting it back together the day she walked away from us because Mia had been dropped at my door. That was why, to this day, I remained single, only having an occasional date here and there. I couldn't allow Mia to get hurt, and allowing women in and out of my life and hers would lead to exactly that.

Scarlett also didn't know I was playing for the Dominators. At least, I hoped she didn't. I'd told her brother not to mention it, but I was certain, with her being in the sports circles, she got notifications of every trade out there. I could only hope she missed the news about mine.

I grabbed my mug and plate and carried it to the kitchen where I was just about to yell down the hall again, when Mia came out of her room carrying her hairbrush.

"Can you brush my hair?" she questioned, shoving

her messy hair out of her face. "Gramma did all summer."

"Mia, honey, we don't have a lot of time," I said, feeling my frustration levels rising.

I'd been in Vancouver for almost eight months. During that time, Mom and Dad had taken Mia for me, which made it easier for me to find a place, a nanny, and get settled in with the team. I'd gone to pick her up last weekend right before the season started, and while we'd had to get used to a new routine again, I was glad to have her back with me, even if it meant being a few minutes late for practice. This morning I'd planned to introduce my little nugget to the guys on the team for the first time.

"I can't go out like this!" she cried while I picked her up and placed her on the stool at the breakfast bar.

"Okay, okay. Let me have the brush."

I took the brush from her and carefully ran it through her long hair, doing my best not to hurt her as I brushed out the tangles. Then, like my mother had taught me, I braided her hair and lifted her down off the stool she was sitting on.

"Thanks, Dad," she said, running off toward her room.

"Okay, get your bag. We've got to go," I called, glancing at my watch again.

She came running out of her room, her little pink

backpack on her back. She came right over to the door, where she slipped on her matching pink running shoes.

"Got everything?" I asked. "Snacks, juice box, crayons, and coloring book?"

"Yep, but I thought there was a playground where we're going."

"There is, don't you worry, you will have a blast. Daddy will be right down on the ice while you're at daycare. If you want, you can even watch me skate around the rink from where you'll be."

"Why can't I come skate with you?"

"You will one day, but not this morning. I have practice. Alright?"

She nodded her head and slipped her small hand into mine while I opened the door. I waited for her to walk out before I hoisted my hockey bag up off the floor, threw it over my shoulder, and pulled the door shut behind me.

MIA STOOD beside me while I emptied my gear out of my bag and into my locker. By some miracle we were early, and since the daycare area wasn't open yet, we'd come down to the locker room to unpack my bag before taking her back there and dropping her off. She sat on the bench in front of me, swinging her legs as she sang along to some song she was making up.

I looked over at her and chuckled to myself as she hummed along, pausing and glancing over her shoulder as she heard a roar of laughter coming down the hall. She glanced up at me with worried eyes as the door opened and the guys poured into the locker room.

"Then I swear I just about died as she got down on her fucking knees and—"

"Hey, whoa!" I yelled, quickly covering Mia's ears as I looked over at Colton, who was probably halfway through telling the guys about his escapades over the weekend.

The guys all stopped in their tracks, questioning looks on their faces as they looked over at me with my hands covering Mia's ears.

"Younger sister?" Colton questioned, dropping his bag, a sly smile on his face.

I hadn't told the guys about Mia. The fact I'd kept her hidden from them wasn't something I was proud of. I'd just needed a break from being a dad for those eight months that my parents had her, so I could be reminded what it was like to not have such an immense responsibility hanging over my head every single second.

It probably would have been easier had they kept her during game time instead of off-season, but this was just as well. It gave me time to seek someone to watch her while I was at practice and game time, and for when I was on the road.

I cleared my throat and removed my hands from her ears.

"Mia, I'd like you to meet some of my teammates," I said, kneeling so I could see her face. "That's Dylan, Knox, Lucas, Clay, and the big guy over there is Colton."

She eyed each one of them with a curious expression, then raised her little hand in a wave, smiling over at Colton.

"Hey, Mia," they all said in unison and then looked at me, questions in their eyes.

"This is my daughter, and we are late for daycare. Come on, sweetie, let's go," I added, not giving one of them a chance to ask me anything while she was with me.

PURPLE LIGHTS SHONE all around the arena as we crashed into one another on our first win of the season. The crowd screamed as music blared over the speakers. It had been a tense game, especially playing against my old team, the New York Predators.

We moved to do our post-game handshake, and when I got to Connor Bailey, he leaned into me.

"Hey, Anderson! How are you doing? You know Scottie is here, right?"

I looked over at him. Connor had been there for me after Scarlett tore my heart into pieces. He also knew I was still very close to Scottie. Scarlett not so much.

"No, he never mentioned he was coming out here," I said, slowing down as the other players moved off the ice.

"She's here too," he whispered and nodded toward the crowd. "Somewhere up there."

"I know, but thanks for the warning," I said, slapping him on his back as I looked up into the area of the crowd above our bench that he'd gestured at.

I moved off the ice without looking up. If she was right there, I didn't want to make eye contact. It was bad enough she'd know who I was playing for now, even though she probably already did.

"I heard you were giving her an interview tonight?" he questioned, stopping before heading toward the away team's dressing room.

"No, I uh, I asked not to be interviewed. Besides I

need to get home to Mia. Listen, we'll catch up soon. I have to run."

"Sure thing, man, give her a little peck for me. Miss that kid. See you later!"

"Later!" I called after him as I made my way down toward our locker room.

Most of the guys on the team had taken off right after they had changed so they could get to the interview on time. I'd taken my time, took a hot shower and, once I was dressed, I grabbed my jacket and keys.

I made my way down the hallway and to our private entrance. I shoved it open and stepped out into the covered parking garage, the cool fall air hitting me in the face. I began heading toward my car when I heard someone say my name.

I turned around, and that was when I saw her step into the light. She looked the same, her dark hair styled the same way she wore it six years ago. She looked sexy as hell in the form-fitting beige suit she wore. I couldn't stop my eyes from skimming over her body before they landed back on her face.

"Levi Anderson. So, I heard it through the grapevine that you refused to allow me to interview you tonight?" she questioned, taking a step forward.

How the hell had she found that out, I wondered to myself. I'd gone to Pamela in private. Perhaps she was only saying that, since it was probably known in her circles I didn't like to give interviews.

"If I'd have been asked, the interview would have been yours," I answered, tripping over my words.

"I see. So, you aren't ignoring me?"

"Of course not. Why would I ignore you?" I questioned.

"For the same reason you've been ignoring me for the past six years—because of that morning," she said, taking another step closer. "Because you're still angry with me."

Scarlett had always been my weakness. She'd always been the one I'd done everything for and the one I'd thought would never ever walk away from me, so when she did exactly that after the woman, I'd had a one-night stand with appeared with my child, it had ruined me. I wouldn't call it angry—hurt and broken-hearted would have been more like it.

"I'm not angry, Scarlett. I'm sure you had your reasons for walking away. I declined the interview for one simple reason: I just don't give interviews."

"You just said, had you of been asked, the interview would have been mine."

"I meant maybe—maybe it would have been yours," I corrected and cleared my throat, running my fingers through my hair. "Besides, I'm just getting settled with the team and in this area, and I've decided

I want to keep a low profile for now. Let Mia get settled into school and adjust to living here without a lot of fanfare."

Scarlett glanced at her watch and then softly smiled.

"How is Mia?" She questioned, looking down at the ground.

"She's good." I said, glancing at my watch, which made Scarlett look at hers.

"Well, Levi, it was good seeing you. Don't be a stranger, okay?"

I frowned. A stranger? Was she serious? She lived in New York, and she was the one who'd made it more than perfectly clear that there was no chance of us having any type of relationship the very last time we spoke.

"Good luck with everything. It was nice seeing you."

I watched as she turned away and entered the building. I don't know why I stood there for a moment, maybe I was waiting for her to return, but when I realized what I was doing I shook my head, turned and made my way to my car.

I STEPPED off the ice the next morning breathless and sat down on the bench. Thank God for breaks I thought to myself as I grabbed my water bottle and took a drink

I was exhausted. Sleep hadn't been kind to me last night, and neither had my memory. Seeing Scarlett again had only reminded me of the memories I'd worked so hard to forget. I reached into my bag and grabbed my granola bar, ripped the wrapper, and took a bite as I watched the rest of the team continue with drills.

"Looking good out there, buddy," I heard a voice say, and turned to see Scottie leaning over the boards from behind me.

"Hey, man. How are you?" I questioned, glad to see my best friend.

"Good. Thought I'd come check out your practice like I used to, so I could see what it is I'm missing out on."

I chuckled. Scottie had played hockey with me while growing up, but an ankle injury early in one of our college games had ended his would-be career.

"Good to see you. How come you didn't tell me you were coming out here? How's Monica?" I asked.

"Wouldn't know, man, she left me," Scottie said, looking a bit defeated.

"Oh no, I'm sorry to hear that." I knew they'd

been having issues, but the last time I heard from Scottie, they were working through them.

"Doesn't matter. Anyway, I wasn't planning on coming. It was Scarlett who dragged me out here, claiming I needed to get out of the house."

I studied Scottie for a minute before he continued. "Scarlett's moving out here. She's being transferred to the Canadian division of the *Ice Insiders*. She's worked her way up, and she is diving in for a promotion with the company."

"Good for her," I said, knowing I didn't mean a word of what I'd just said, while taking another drink.

"Yeah, I'm proud of her. She's gone after what she wanted, and it's gotten her far, just like you said it would."

"That's good, man. I'm happy for her," I said, leaning back against the bench, watching my team members on the ice. "Still doesn't explain why she made you come all the way here. Figured Duncan would have brought her," I answered.

Her leaving had gutted me and then came the next blow. I'm not sure which had been worse, her leaving, or what happened in the following months. Duncan, one of her college friends, had moved right on in after we'd gone our separate ways. I'd always known he'd had something for her, and even though I'd gone after her after she walked away from me and tried to get her to come back to me, she'd refused. She kept telling me that Mia, work, and learning how to deal with being a single dad were my priorities and that they should be the only things on my mind.

"He would have, but—"

"Scottie, it doesn't matter, I don't care." I said, stopping him before he could continue.

Scottie looked at me, something hidden in his expression. As far as I was concerned, the ship that Scarlett and I had once sailed on was long gone, as was friendship or any other type of relationship.

"Mom was worried about her, so she asked me to come out here with her while she got settled in her new place."

"How long are you staying for?" I questioned, wanting to get off the topic of Scarlett.

"Tonight's my last night."

"Heading back to New York?"

"Yes, work only allowed me so much time off between the divorce and this impromptu trip."

"I get that. Well, maybe the next time you're out here we can get together."

Scottie nodded, then leaned forward. "Levi, before I go, I wanted to ask you something."

"Shoot," I said, still watching the team on the ice.

"Would you mind keeping an eye on Scarlett?"

I choked on the mouthful of water I'd just taken

and looked at Scottie, disbelief no doubt present on my face. Was he serious? Was he seriously asking me to watch out for her? We'd been down this road once before, and I wasn't about to run down it again. Plus, she had Duncan.

"You two used to be so close, and I know she is going to need someone she can trust, especially living this far away from home… Please Levi."

"Key word in that sentence was 'used to be,' Scottie. Things changed the day she walked out that door. And between Mia, practices, and my game schedule, I can't add on driving out to another part of the city and checking on her. I barely have the energy to make it to my bed at night now that Mia is back with me." I chuckled.

"What if I told you that you wouldn't have to go far?"

Again, I chuckled. "That still wouldn't make a difference, man. A city block would be too far most days. She'll be fine on her own," I said, watching as Coach Thompkins waved me back on the ice. "Look, I've got to get back out there. We'll talk later, and I hope you get Scarlett all settled in before you have to go back to the city. I'm sure Duncan will look after his princess once he gets here."

Scottie nodded, saying nothing more about the topic. "Alright, man, good luck out there."

I was just about to put my foot back on the ice but turned back to Scottie. "Just know had things of ended a little differently between her and I, I'd be there for her in a heartbeat. I just can't go back down that path, man," I said, feeling bad for my answer.

"Hey, no hard feelings. I was out of line to even ask."

"It was good to see you." I nodded and then took off onto the ice, skating away from Scottie and my past, and looked toward my present day.

Chapter Three

Scarlett - Two Weeks Later

Sweat poured from my brow as I ran down the side street near the water. I loved my morning runs, and it made it even better to have the beautiful scenery of this new city.

I was on my last leg. Only one more street to go, I thought as I stopped at the traffic light, jogging in place until the light turned. The moment I had permission to cross, I proceeded, heading up the street, and I slowed my pace as I approached the building.

The tall thirty-story condo was my new home. One I loved. I'd even met some nice people since moving in, especially my neighbour Mrs. Fletcher, a sixty-five-year-old recently widowed lady who lived in the unit across the hall from me. Just as I made it to the base of the walkway, I looked up to see her leaving the building.

"Morning, Scarlett. How was your run, dear?" she greeted.

"Good, as always. It's a beautiful day too, so that didn't hurt," I said, smiling.

"One of the last few I take it. It will turn cold soon."

"I know. Good thing I'm used to harsh winters." I smiled. "You off to your card game?" I asked, stretching out my calf muscle.

I'd lived here less than three weeks and already knew her schedule—probably better than she did. She not only played cards three mornings a week with the gin club, but she also worked as a nanny to one tenant in the building. Five years ago, she'd lost her husband of thirty years to a massive stroke. It was that story that had intrigued me. We'd shared dinner, and that was when I'd told her about Duncan.

She listened quietly and then grabbed hold of my hand and told me I had a whole life ahead of me, that I needed to work through his loss, pack up that sorrow and find myself one of the eligible bachelors in the building. I only smiled, then laughed, telling her I was ready to date again.

"You know it, dear. Those buggers stole sixty from

me last week in what I like to call a fake hand, so I'm going in guns blazing and get my money back."

"You get them." I laughed.

"Plan on it. Oh, and have you, by chance, run into any of the eligible bachelors we talked about?"

I smiled and shook my head. "Not yet. My co-worker has decided I should try a blind date with her friend first. Then I promise I'll look."

"You make sure you do if the blind date doesn't work out. There are some very well-off ones in this building, not to mention some very attractive ones too," she said, waving her hand in front of her face. "There is even one of the hockey players from the Dominators in the building. I know him very well, so, if you'd like an introduction, all you need to do is ask. He's a lovely young man, by the way, and his daughter is a special little something."

My body flooded with heat at the mention of the team. There was no doubt they were all attractive, but one hockey player in my lifetime was probably enough, I thought to myself.

"I'll keep that in mind. Thanks." I smiled as a cab pulled up.

"Alright, dear, wish me luck."

"Good luck," I said, waving, and made my way into the building and over to the elevator where I pushed the button and then leaned against the wall.

My watch vibrated, notifying me of an email. I quickly navigated to see who it was from and was surprised to see my boss, Carol, had messaged me about our Monday morning meeting. As I read through the email, excitement built in me. She wanted to see me alone after the usual team meeting Monday morning.

I pushed myself off the wall and made my way over to the mailboxes, checking to see if I had any mail while I was down here. I pulled the small stack of envelopes from the tiny box and turned back around, coming face to chest with someone.

"Oh my, I'm sorry, I didn't…" I stopped speaking when I looked up to see who was standing before me.

"Scarlett?" What are you…" Levi muttered, his hands full of grocery bags.

"Levi, funny meeting you here," I said.

"Not really, since I live here."

My heart raced as I stared back at him. It didn't matter how much time had passed. He still did that to me, making my heart race. It was beating out of my chest the other night when I ran into him at the arena too, actually causing me to become lightheaded for a few seconds after we parted ways.

As we stood there looking at one another, I had a sudden urge to pour my heart out to him, to tell him everything that had happened since we'd split, and how I regretted my choice more than he'd ever know, but there was no way I could give in that easily.

"I live here too," I mumbled.

Levi looked at me, then swallowed hard before he nodded. "I see. Well, I guess welcome to the building," he said, looking anywhere but my eyes.

My stomach tightened while I thought about the pair of us living in the same building. I'd worried when Mrs. Fletcher mentioned that a Dominator lived in the building with his daughter that it might be Levi but quickly passed it off. I figured there was no way it would be him.

"Thanks. I think."

Our eyes locked as we stood there, neither of us saying anything. Was this how it was going to be between us forever? Were we even capable of going back to how things had once been between us?

"Well, it was nice seeing you. I have to get these groceries upstairs. Ice-cream you know," he said, lifting the bags. "See you around," he muttered, heading to the now open elevator doors. "Are you coming?"

I shook my head. "No, I think I'm going to head back out and do another run," I lied.

"Alright, suit yourself," he said.

The moment those doors closed, I let out the breath I'd been holding and leaned up against the wall again. Out of all the places in Vancouver, how the hell had I picked the building he lived in?

I swallowed hard, moved to the elevator, and hit the button again, once again waiting for it to arrive.

I COVERED my mouth and yawned as I listened while Carol handed out our assignments. I took a sip of my coffee, praying for the caffeine to give me a boost. After all, I was going on less than five hours of sleep a night again for the third week in a row.

"Are we keeping you awake, Scarlett?" Carol asked, looking in my direction.

"Sorry, I guess I've been burning the candle at both ends."

She said nothing and turned her attention back to the team. Once she handed out all the assignments and dismissed everyone, she turned to me.

"Scarlett, I'd like to talk to you before you start your day. Do you have a couple of minutes?"

I straightened and nodded. "Of course," I said, taking a seat at the large boardroom table.

"Scarlett, this article on the Dominators' games last week couldn't have been more perfect. In fact, you captured the excitement from the team so perfectly, better than any other articles I've read."

"Thanks, I did the best I could."

"It shows, and with that comes rewards. I've decided that I want you in charge of their specific division on the *Insiders'* publication. You will cover every game, be it here or away."

"Wow, really? Thank you, I'm beyond excited." I said, perking up.

"I'm glad. Now, that means that for each game here in the city starting in two weeks, you will have front row access. You will also travel, so get ready for a busy season."

"I'll be traveling?"

"Yes, now it won't be to every away game, but for the bigger games, you will definitely be on the road."

"I see." I swallowed hard.

How the hell was I going to explain this to Levi? He'd think I was stalking him. In fact, it would look that way to anyone who knew we'd had a history.

My heart sped up as I watched her pull out a folder and shuffle through the papers inside. She set a pile off to the side, shuffled through a few more, setting more in another pile, and then stopped and looked down at the two papers left in her hand.

"I am sure you're wondering what I was doing there," she said, resting her chin on her hands.

"Perhaps," I said, swallowing hard as I placed my pen down on my notebook.

"You're going to want that." She nodded at the pen.

Immediately, I grabbed it and got ready to write what she was going to say. For some reason, I had an icky feeling in the pit of my stomach from the look on her face. I twirled my pen as I sat there waiting for her to start.

"As I am sure you are probably aware, there are two players who are rather new to the Dominators, only having completed playing half a season with the team. Colton Fox and Levi Anderson."

I lifted my head and looked at Carol, who sat there staring at me as she shoved the biographies of both the players toward me. I picked up the papers, looked at them, and nodded.

"Yes, both players were transferred at the middle to end of the season last year. Traded to the team."

"Correct, however, I'm not sure that you've noticed, but most of the Dominators players, especially the starting lineup, are always in the news. Dylan Hayes, Knox Evans, Lucas Clark, and Clay Harris are all rather outgoing in the media and take part in many social programs. While Clay doesn't provide many interviews, Levi Anderson and Colton Fox take hardly any."

"Well, that could be for many reasons," I said, but Carol held her hand up to stop me.

"Colton Fox has a reputation. I'd hedge a guess that is why he's been off-limits to many personal and private interviews. However, he often appears in the news regarding whatever latest scandal he is involved with."

"I can see what I can do about getting an interview with him if you'd like," I offered, hoping to avoid the Levi situation.

Carol smiled and then shook her head.

"I'd love a personal and private interview with each of the players, but to be honest, Clay and Colton are not the ones I'm interested in."

"They aren't?"

"No. What I am interested in is Levi."

"Levi?" I repeated.

"Yes. The others have given personal interviews—few, but they still give them—but Levi has never."

I swallowed hard. It was true. Levi hated being in the public eye. I knew that from when he first got signed. I remembered that he immediately refused to speak to any journalist, even going so far as getting his lawyer to remove the publicity clause from his contract. He told me about it, and even though the clause had stayed in his contract, everyone knew it was a section that was void.

So, I knew how Levi felt about interviews; he didn't want the fanfare for being a skilled player. He loved the sport, and he loved playing it, and in his mind, fanfare was something that could ruin it for him. Then, when Mia came along, it became something else entirely, or so I'd heard from Scottie.

"I want the *Ice Insiders* to be the first publication to have an interview with him. He is a hell of a player, and I want us to be the first to—"

I tapped my pencil on the table and looked at Carol as she stared back at me.

"Is there a problem?" she questioned.

"No, not at all," I said, remembering that Levi had told me that had I asked him for the interview, he would have granted me one, so maybe that meant that he'd trust me to run the interview.

"You look like you are going to be sick," she said.

"No, just been feeling a little off because of the lack of sleep. Just leave it with me and I'll see what I can do." I smiled, closing my notebook and shoving it back into my bag.

I got up and walked to the door when Carol cleared her throat.

"Scarlett…"

I turned around. "Yes."

"You do this for me, you get this interview with Levi this season, no matter how long it takes, and I will make sure that you get that promotion you're after," she said.

I studied her expression. Was she bribing me?

"Whatever it takes, Scarlett. You get me that interview, and I promise you the job is yours."

I WAS EXHAUSTED by the time I pulled my car into my parking space behind the building. I'd barely got any work done after my meeting with Carol because I hadn't been able to stop thinking about everything that was said.

I climbed out of my car, grabbed my bag from the back seat, then reached in and grabbed the rest of my cup of coffee from an hour ago. With my bag flung over my shoulder, coffee in hand, I walked with my head down as I checked my phone for messages.

I'd just turned the corner when I tripped over something. I flew forward, trying to maintain my balance and keep the coffee in my hand from spilling, when I felt myself bang right into someone and then felt the warm liquid travel down my blouse.

"Ugh, oh god!" I cried as I looked down at the mess of my new white silk blouse.

"Fuck me…why don't you watch—" I heard a male voice say.

I closed my eyes for a brief second, knowing exactly who belonged to that voice.

I looked up to see Levi staring back at me in anger, coffee down the front of his white dress shirt.

Embarrassment filled my face as I stared at him, feeling bad for making such a mess of the pair of us.

"Dad, we aren't supposed to say fuck," I heard a small voice say and looked down to see little Mia staring up at me, her hair and clothes coffee-covered as well. When she turned her eyes back to me, I could see how unimpressed she was that he'd sworn.

"I'm so sorry. I was checking my email," I cried, pulling my blouse from my skirt and wiping Mia's face with the front of it so she didn't get coffee in her eyes.

"No worries, lady. It's just like being in the shower. Dad sometimes swears then too." She giggled as her large blue eyes looked up at me.

I glanced up to see Levi glaring at me.

I awkwardly smiled at him and shrugged my shoulders. "I'm sorry."

"Sorry doesn't help the fact that we are running late. Nor does it help that we will surely be late now that I'm going to have to take her back upstairs, clean her up, and get her dressed again, along with myself.

I looked down at Mia, who stood there looking up at both of us, a grin on her face.

"It's okay, Daddy."

"It's not okay, Mia," he grumbled as he stared at me.

"Don't be mad at the pretty lady, Daddy. It was an accident."

While Scottie had shown me pictures over the years of Mia, they hadn't done her justice. She was the cutest little thing I'd ever seen. So cute, in fact, that my heart hurt even more now knowing I'd separated myself from Levi intentionally because I thought it would be easier for him to focus on his daughter without me in his life. I never cared that he had a baby dropped in his lap from some girl who was certain he was the father. I didn't care that he'd had a one-night stand while I was in school. I didn't care because I loved him, always had, and if I thought about it, still did.

"Okay, look, how about I make it up to you?" I asked.

"How are you going to do that?" he scoffed. "Do you have any more coffee you wish to drop on us before we go get cleaned up and changed?"

I bit my bottom lip, trying not to snap back at him. His comment wasn't fair. It truly had been an accident.

"Well, I am supposed to have a date tonight, but I

will cancel. Since I know you are running late, I could look after Mia while you head to your game? I could get her cleaned up and feed her dinner, maybe take her to see the new Disney movie that's playing."

Levi looked at me as if I'd lost my mind. While I hadn't seen him in a long time, I still wasn't a stranger, and I'd babysat plenty of kids growing up. He should know he could trust me.

"I don't think so," he said, clearing his throat, then looked down at Mia, who was pulling on his arm. "What is it?" he asked.

"Daddy, how does she know my name?" she asked, giving me a curious look.

"Don't worry about it," he said, placing his hand on her shoulder.

"No, how does she know my name? I don't know her," Mia questioned, looking up at me.

I knew Levi would probably hate me, but I knelt down and came eye level with Mia and smiled softly. "I'm a friend of your dad's, one from a long time ago."

"How come I've never seen you before?"

"Well, I guess that is because I didn't live here before."

"Where did you live?"

"In New York. I've known your dad for a long time."

Mia looked up at Levi. "She lives in New York, just

like Uncle Scottie," she said, jumping up and down with excitement.

Levi didn't entertain anymore of the conversation between Mia and me. Instead, he gripped her shoulder and turned her toward the front door of the building, leaving me bent down on the sidewalk.

"We've got to go or I'm going to be late," he grumbled as he opened the door to the building.

Mia stopped, looked back at me and then up at Levi. "Daddy, why are you being so grumpy? You tell me when I'm grumpy I have to go to my room."

I couldn't help but smile as I caught the annoyed look on Levi's face.

"Mia, I said let's go," he said, his voice taking on a firmer tone.

"I don't want to go," she said, pulling her hand from his and crossing her arms.

"Mia, I don't have the time for this. Let's go."

"No." She stomped her foot and looked over at me. "I want to stay with her." She yelled, running toward me, but Levi caught her before she got to me.

Picking her up, he threw her over his shoulder and opened the door to the building walking inside just as she let out a blood-curdling scream.

"Mia, I've had enough," I heard him growl just as the door of the building closed.

I followed them inside and waited beside them while we waited for the elevator.

"Seriously, Levi, I can look after her. It's not a problem."

"I don't think so. To be honest, you've done enough, but thanks for the offer," he barked, just as the elevator door opened and we both stepped inside. Levi hit the twenty-ninth floor and then looked at me, waiting. "Well?"

"Thirteenth," I answered, holding my bag in front of me, not saying another word until we got to my floor.

"Night," I said, stepping out of the elevator.

"Enjoy your date. Say hello to Duncan for me," Levi muttered as he pressed the button to close the elevator doors.

The sound of Duncan's name rolling off Levi's lips took me by surprise. I'd figured Scottie would have told him what had happened, but he'd apparently left that out.

I let out the breath I was holding and made my way down the corridor to my unit. Just when I hadn't thought it was possible for this day to get any worse, it did.

Chapter Four

Levi

"Fucking amazing!" Colton shouted as we headed down the hallway toward the locker room at the end of the game. "That's how we fucking play!"

"Sure is. That was an absolutely amazing shot, Levi," Dylan said, smacking me on the shoulder. "We really should take tonight and head out to celebrate. Our fifth win out of five games and all."

"You guys go ahead," Clay said, dropping onto the bench in the locker room. "I told Peyton I'd be home after the game."

"Killjoy!" Lucas chuckled.

"No, not a killjoy. I just promised I'd be there to be with her tonight."

Knox pulled his jersey off and nodded. "That's right, he needs to stand up to the words he promised me. To look after her," he said, giving him the same look he'd given him the night he'd found out they were together, only to laugh the moment Clay did.

I could still hear the crowd cheering as I took off my jersey and dumped it into the laundry hamper in the corner.

"Well, I'm down. I just need to check in with Mrs. Fletcher and make sure Mia is okay."

Once I'd gotten back to our place, Mia had a full-on meltdown because I'd refused to let her stay with Scarlett. I'd called Mrs. Fletcher in a panic, knowing full well I'd not be able to get her calmed down, cleaned up, and ready in time to make it to the game. She came right up to my place, and before I left, she had things under control and Mia in a warm bath. It was a blessing that she lived in the building for emergencies just like this. I seriously did not know just how lucky I'd been when I'd found her.

I grabbed my phone and quickly called her. The moment I mentioned going out with the guys she confirmed everything was okay and told me to have a wonderful time. Moments later, I'd gotten out of my gear and was on my way to the showers.

"So where do you guys want to go? Illusions? Tilted Flask? I'd suggest The Rusty Anchor, but it's game night."

When I turned around, I saw Knox staring at me with an annoyed look on his face, shaking his head.

"What?" I asked.

"Don't you know by now that if I'm going out with all of you, we go to Illusions?"

I held up my hands in front of me and chuckled. "Sorry there, big guy. I guess our decision has been made. Illusions it is." I laughed.

I STOOD in our private room, a drink in my hand, looking down over the dance floor while the guys behind me stood talking about the game.

"I can't believe you were so late tonight," Dylan said, coming up beside me. "When I messaged you, you said you were on your way. I got a little worried when you didn't show up on time."

"Yeah, well, there was a bit of a mishap with a cup of coffee and one careless woman who wasn't paying attention," I said, grabbing a slice of pizza from the tray before Lucas returned it to the table.

"Doesn't sound too good."

"It wasn't, and when I went to take Mia back to the condo to get her cleaned up, she had a full-on meltdown. If it hadn't of been for Mrs. Fletcher, I'd have missed tonight." I sighed, taking a bite of my pizza.

"So, who was hell on feet?" Dylan chuckled as he grabbed a slice of pizza from the tray.

"Remember Scarlett Green?" I questioned. "The reporter from the *Ice Insiders*?"

"Yeah."

"Fucking reporters. Get her the fuck out of here, Tommy!" Colton yelled, grabbing both of our attention.

We both turned and looked in time to see Colton come back into the room, looking seriously annoyed and pissed off.

"What the hell is going on?" Dylan asked, looking over at Colton and Knox as they stood talking to one another.

"That fucking reporter from the *Insiders*. She followed me through the club, demanding an interview now. Almost got up here if it hadn't of been for John at the bottom of the stairs. They go overboard when they are fucking desperate." Colton huffed, taking a cold beer that Lucas had ready. "That's the reason I hate doing interviews."

Irritation and worry flooded me as I looked over

my shoulder and quietly scanned the dance floor. It took me a minute, but I finally spotted Scarlett in the centre of the dance floor with a couple of girls, dancing and laughing. Then a man approached her, handed her a drink, and placed his hand on the small of her back, joining in the conversation.

"I told Tommy to have her forcibly removed if necessary. None of us are going to be harassed because we need to take a piss."

"I'll call Pamela, ask for a meeting, then we'll notify her of this," Dylan said, pulling his phone from his pocket. "They won't have the opportunity for another interview if I have my way."

"Good thinking," Knox added. "I already had to call once last week because one reporter followed Lorelai through the grocery store and out to her car."

"Jesus, better tell all the girls to watch their backs," Dylan added.

"I'll be back," I mumbled as I made my way out the door and down to the dance floor. I would not allow her to do this.

Anger flooded me as I made my way through the crowd. I had no clue what I was going to say to her once I got to her, but she needed to know she crossed the line.

People bumped into me as I made my way through the crowd. I went straight for the location I'd seen her in earlier, only to find she wasn't there. Looking around, I finally spotted her over at one of the small side bars with the two girls. I made my way over to where she stood and tapped her on the shoulder. She whipped around and looked at me.

"Levi?" she questioned. "What are you doing here?" She smiled.

"Don't you dare pretend like you didn't know I was here. Who do you think you are?"

A stunned look came over her face as I waited for her answer.

"I…I do not know what you're talking about. I'm here on my date," she said through clenched teeth.

"Yeah, right. That is why you followed Colton through the bar, begging him for an interview," I barked. "Are you that fucking desperate for an interview? I take it you are probably up for a promotion and are looking for a fast way to get one?"

"Levi," she cried, holding her hands up in front of her, "I'd never do that."

"So, you're going to lie to me. Colton already told me. He's in the process of having you removed from the bar, forcibly if it comes to it. If you want an interview, then go through the proper channels."

She looked up at me, tears welling in the corner of her eyes as I continued to glare at her. Part of me wanted to apologize immediately, because I knew that her crying told me she wasn't lying to me. I swallowed hard, debating what to do as she looked at me, when a man, about my height, came up to her and placed his hand on the small of her back.

"Everything okay here, Scarlett?" he asked, giving me a once-over.

I swallowed hard. That wasn't Duncan, I thought to myself, not that it was any of my business who she was here with. Perhaps shit hadn't worked out between them. I didn't know, nor did I really care.

Scarlett glared at me and then turned and looked at the man beside her. "Everything is fine. Let's go dance," she said, wrapping her arm around his and pulling him away from me.

I stood there watching as they walked away from me and began dancing, confusion filling me. Not that it was any of my business, but she'd gotten engaged to Duncan a little over two years ago. I remembered seeing their announcement in the paper. Not that I stalked her, but I kept my ear to the ground when it concerned her. Plus, despite me asking him not to, Scottie always kept me up to date with what was going on in her life.

I pulled my phone from my pocket and opened a new chat between Scottie and me. I was about to go against everything I'd vowed never to do again.

I remembered when he confirmed their engagement. I sat there staring at my phone, the words blurring as I'd digested the confirmation he'd given me. I waited a few minutes, hurt, anger, and so many other emotions stirring inside me as Mia had cried on my lap. I messaged him back an hour later and told him never to tell me another thing about her again. Anytime he'd bring her up after that, I'd stop him and tell him I didn't care, when in fact my words couldn't have been further from the truth. Of course, over the years when he mentioned her, I'd stopped telling him I didn't want to hear about her.

I stared at the blank screen, at that stupid flashing cursor, and was about to message him when I felt someone poke me in the back. I whipped around to see Dylan and Knox standing there.

"She's gone. Come back up. They just brought more beer. We can eat and drink in peace now. The big guy has calmed," Dylan said, pointing to the door as the two club guards removed a woman.

Regret filled me as I looked over my shoulder and saw Scarlett, still dancing, but now smiling and laughing at whatever the guy she was with said. I was such an ass. I'd jumped to the conclusion it had been her who'd come after Colton.

I shoved my phone into my pocket, turned, and followed Dylan and Knox back upstairs, where I grabbed a beer, sat down on the couch, and decided tonight was going to be the one and only night I'd allow myself to sink deep into all the feelings of regret for letting Scarlett slip away.

IT FELT like someone was taking a hot poker to my brain as Mia let out another loud scream.

"Mia, can you please stop crying?" I moaned.

This was what I got for a night of heavy drinking. One hell of a horrendous headache, and one sick, crying, and very cranky child. I grabbed my mug of cold coffee and took a sip, then took a bite of my bagel, which wasn't sitting very well, and tried to give Mia another spoonful of her oatmeal. She shoved my hand away, causing me to drop the spoon onto the floor. I let out a loud, frustrated sigh and closed my eyes for a moment while rubbing my temples, only to hear her dish smash as it hit the floor.

Oatmeal covered the tile floor, mixed in with pieces of broken glass. I looked at Mia who sat there, her eyes red and full of tears. I lifted her down off the chair and placed her on the floor, clear from the broken bowl.

"Just go into the living room and lie down," I

muttered, grabbing the roll of paper towels and the garbage.

"But…. I'm…. I'm hunnnnngrrrrrrryy," she cried again, stomping her feet on the floor.

I pinched the bridge of my nose and took a deep breath.

"Mia…go lay on the couch and I'll bring you in something when I'm done cleaning up this mess here," I said, my patience wearing thin.

I knew I should have crashed at Colton's last night. He'd offered, but instead of taking him up on that offer because I'd felt bad asking Mrs. Fletcher to stay, I'd come home. When she left, I stupidly told her she could have today off, that I would be fine without her. Normally, she came and stayed with Mia on Sunday while I went out to get groceries and run any other errands I had, but I figured I'd give her the day off since we were travelling later this week, but now that Mia woke with a tiny fever, I was regretting my decision.

Finished cleaning up the mess of oatmeal and glass, I pulled out a pan to make some scrambled eggs for us to share. I was just about to dump the eggs into the pan when my phone went off. Grabbing it, I looked down to see a message from Scottie.

SCOTTIE: What the fuck do you think you are doing? Accusing Scarlett the way you did? What the fuck is the matter with you?

Yep, here it was. This damn day couldn't get much worse, could it? I dumped the eggs into the pan, debating whether to answer him, when my phone went off again.

SCOTTIE: Don't think I'll let you off the hook without an answer.

LEVI: Look, it wasn't my brightest moment, okay. Let's just say I overreacted.

SCOTTIE: Overreacted? You think? Come on, man....I know things haven't exactly gone the way you planned....

LEVI: It was a mistake, Scottie.

SCOTTIE: You owe her an apology. She called me in fucking tears last night when she got home.

LEVI: What about her apology for dumping coffee all over me and Mia yesterday afternoon?

SCOTTIE: That was an accident, and you know it.

LEVI: Fine. Whenever I see her next, I'll apologize.

SCOTTIE: No, you'll make time today to apologize.

I rolled my eyes and threw my phone down on the counter, took my frustration out on the pan of eggs, and poured them onto the plate as I heard my phone go off again. I grabbed it and looked at the message Scottie left.

SCOTTIE: Well?

LEVI: Noted.

Instead of waiting for a response, I shut my phone off, leaving it on the counter, grabbed the eggs and a fork and made my way into the living room where I found Mia sound asleep on the couch.

I covered her with the blanket that lay over the back and sat down in the chair across from her, turning the television off cartoons to the sports channel, sat back, and dug the fork into the plate of eggs, taking my mind off everything else.

Chapter Five

Scarlett

I poured a cup of hot coffee, grabbed my fruit and yogurt, and made my way out to my balcony. It was a gorgeous fall morning; it was too bad my mood didn't reflect the sunshine. I tightened the tie of my bathrobe and then sat down, taking a sip of coffee and shoving a raspberry in my mouth.

Last night had been horrible. The more I thought about it, the more my head ached. My coworker Janice had been on me since I'd arrived out here, and she found out I was single. She claimed she had the most perfect guy for me, but then everyone had said the same thing, and for that reason alone, I'd never agreed to go on any blind date. However, she must have chipped away at my strong exterior just long enough to annoy me because one afternoon I finally broke down and agreed.

Not that he was an awful person, but he wasn't my type, that much I knew the moment I'd met him. First, he brought me roses, and to most women, they'd have loved the flowers. However, I'm deathly allergic, which Janice had known. I'd have probably been fine had I just asked Janice to put them in a vase in her kitchen, but she insisted I smell them, claiming she always did when Eddie, her boyfriend, gave them to her. That started the sneezing.

Once I'd gotten over that and we were at the restaurant, he'd ordered my food for me. If there was one thing I hated more than roses, it was a man who asked me what I was thinking of having, and when I mention I was torn between two dishes, he decided he'd just make that choice for me. Of course, I spoke up and ordered what I wanted anyway, which was the opposite choice he'd picked. It was those two incidents that had set the mood for me for the entire evening.

Once dinner was done, we made our way over to a club called Illusions for dancing and drinks, which, to be honest, I was a little excited about. It had been a long time since I'd been out dancing. We got some drinks and found a perfect spot on the dance floor, and for the first time all night, I was actually having fun.

Until I saw Levi come in with some guys from the team.

I had a hard time keeping my eyes off him, until they all disappeared. I figured they'd left the club, only to find out an hour later I'd been wrong. He approached me out of nowhere, demanding that I leave the team alone. Embarrassment and hurt flooded me as he stood there, accusing me of doing something I'd never do. That was when Paul came to my rescue, but to avoid a scene and a fight that I could already see brewing, I pulled him away, only to have him keep telling me he'd take care of him if I wanted. No matter how many times I told him no, he kept harping on it all evening, including when he dropped me off.

He walked me to the door. I could tell he wanted to come up, but I quickly put an end to that, lying and telling him I had to be up and out the door for work early this morning. Plus, I'd had too much to drink and didn't want the night to end in some mistake I'd end up regretting. Instead, I promised to reach out to him, but I had no intention of ever calling him again, and I could only hope Janice hadn't given him my number.

I shoved a spoonful of yogurt into my mouth, took a sip of coffee, and sat back in my chair, looking out over the water just as my phone chimed with a message.

Picking it up, I was shocked to see Levi's name on my screen. I swallowed hard and my hands shook as I typed my password in and navigated to his message.

LEVI: Sorry.

Anger flooded me. Had my brother messaged Levi this morning after my drunken phone call last night? I wondered. I'd been so upset when I got home that I'd messaged Scottie. I didn't know what else to do; I needed someone to talk to, to vent to. I'd spilled it all—about the horrific coffee accident and then about Levi accusing me of going after the players on the team to get an interview off company time. It probably hadn't been the best idea, but I was hurting. That wasn't the only reason I was hurting. It was the anniversary of Duncan's accident, which seemed to magnify everything.

I dialed Scottie's number and waited for him to answer. The moment I heard his voice, I jumped right in.

"Did you happen to message Levi and tell him to apologize?"

"Damn right I did. There was no way he should have accused you the way he did."

"I don't need you to fight my battles for me, Scottie."

"I never said you did, but I also know that with Levi Anderson, you wouldn't say anything about it, either."

"Are you saying I wouldn't stand up for myself?" I asked, picking at my cuticle as embarrassment flooded my body.

"That's exactly what I'm saying."

"Why would you say that?"

"Because it's the truth. You never did with him."

"That's because I never had to!" I cried.

That part was true. There had never been a day in my life since I'd met Levi that I ever had to stand up for myself. Our relationship never worked that way. We didn't do things to one another that hurt the other. We never had to apologize or mention that we didn't like the way the other person was treating them, because we never took the other for granted. It was as if we had a mutual understanding between us, until, well, until that morning.

"I beg to differ. I think had you of stood up for yourself to start with when you wanted to date him, you'd have been with him now."

This was the problem with being close to your brother and sharing your thoughts and feelings, I thought to myself. He'd seen me agonize over the fact that Levi wouldn't commit to me until I'd graduated from school. Even though it bothered me, I'd never voiced my disappointment or disagreement with him.

"That's your opinion, but I'm going to remind you that his reason for not dating me was because of you."

"I'm not getting into this with you again. I'm only going to say that he can't treat you like that, Scarlett. You did nothing, and his behaviour crossed a line I didn't like. So, therefore, he should be and will apologize to you. Did he come down and talk to you?"

I pulled my phone away from my ear and looked at the text Levi had sent. I still hadn't responded. I debated how I was going to answer him when I heard him clear his throat.

"Well? Did he?"

"Yep, he did. It's fine. I just don't want you fighting my battles for me," I said, hearing a knock in the distance.

I got up off my chair and stepped into my condo, only to hear another knock at the door.

"Good, I'm glad. Now, if you don't want me to interfere, then stand up for yourself."

"I've got to go. I'll call you later."

"Talk later."

I ended the call and walked over to the door of my condo, looking through the peephole. I immediately stepped back when I saw who it was. I looked down at myself, wrapped in my silk lavender-colored bathrobe, and let out a sigh. I closed my eyes, unlocked the door, and then opened it to come face-to-face with Levi. He wore a pair of faded and ripped jeans, and a Dominator's T-shirt, along with a Vancouver Grizzlies baseball hat backwards over his dark hair. He stood there, hands in his pockets, staring at me.

"Can we talk?" he questioned.

I looked around the hallway for Mia.

"Aren't you missing someone?"

"It would appear that way. She's upstairs with her nanny. I have some errands to run, and since she isn't feeling too well, I figured it was best she stay home. Anyway, I wanted to stop in. Do you have a couple of minutes?" he asked again, his eyes falling down my body, then back up to my eyes.

"Sure, as you can see, I'm not dressed for any type of adventure. Come in," I said, stepping to the side and waiting while he entered.

I shut the door behind him, turning to find he'd made his way into the living room. My heart was racing and the room suddenly felt very warm, although I'd left the sliding door open.

I followed him and was just about to him when he stopped walking and turned, causing me to stop as well. Our eyes locked, neither of us saying anything. I cleared my throat.

"What is it?" I questioned, crossing my arms over my chest.

"Look, first, I want to apologize for last night. I'm sorry for accusing you."

I nodded. "Don't worry about it," I replied, trying not to act like his actions had bothered me. "Anything else?"

Levi looked at me. I could tell he wanted to say something else, but he said nothing.

"What?" I asked.

"What, what?" he repeated.

"You want to know something, I can tell," I said.

"Who was the guy?"

I frowned as I met his eyes, and then I turned away from him.

"He was a blind date," I answered.

When I turned around, I could see him running things over in his mind. I knew he'd known about Duncan and me. Hell, it had been all over the papers when we'd gotten engaged. After all, Duncan had been a high-powered lawyer in New York, working at one of the biggest law firms that represented the owners of the New York Predators

"I see. Where is Duncan? Didn't things work out?"

He didn't know? How was that possible? Sure, he'd already transferred to Vancouver by the time it happened, but I was certain that one of his friends on the old team would have mentioned it. If not, Scottie would have said something, plus it had been all over the papers.

"I doubt he'd be okay with you being on some stupid blind date."

"Things didn't work out," I answered, not giving up any more information than that. He hadn't been a part of my life for so long, I didn't feel the need to answer him with the truth of what had really happened.

"I'm sorry to hear that, Scarlett."

"Are you?" I questioned.

"Am I what?"

"Sorry?"

"Yes, Scarlett, I'm sorry. Things may not have worked between us, but that doesn't mean I would wish you a world of pain, either," he said, shoving his hands back into his pockets. "I'm not some asshole, you know."

"I'm sorry. You didn't deserve that."

He studied me. "No, I didn't."

He turned away from me and walked over to the patio door, glancing outside to see where I'd left my breakfast and coffee. Then he turned back to me. "So, did the date go well?"

Was he seriously asking me how it went last night?

"He's not my type," I muttered, moving to the couch and sitting down.

"I see. Well, maybe you should get yourself settled in the city before you jump into the dating scene," he said, leaning up against one of my armchairs.

"Is that so?"

"Yeah. One can't be too careful, new city and all."

"I'll keep that in mind," I said, crossing my arms over my chest.

"Perhaps it might be better if you didn't date anyone at all," he added.

I frowned. "What is that supposed to mean?"

"Exactly what I said. Put your focus elsewhere."

"On what?"

Levi shrugged. "I don't know, a new hobby, crossing ten more items off of that bucket list you used to carry around, or me?"

A flood of shock washed over me as I looked at him. Where the hell was this coming from? I stood up and began pacing back and forth. Was he really suggesting what I thought he was suggesting? That we see one another again? He couldn't be, I thought. I glanced over to see him standing there, his arms crossed in front of his chest.

"Levi, that is not a good idea," I said, my voice shaking.

"What isn't? The bucket list?" He asked, smirking in my direction.

"I was referring to the last part of your suggestion."

"Why am I not a good idea?" he asked.

"What do you mean, why not? Have you completely lost your mind?"

"No, I meant exactly what I said I'm single, you're apparently single and wanting to date. I know what the guys are like in this town…and I at least know if you're dating me, you aren't out with some jackass."

"You do?"

"Yes, so the way I look at it, problems are solved."

"Your focus shouldn't be on me, Levi. You have Mia to worry about and look after."

"Ah, yes, once again, Mia, your favorite excuse. Newsflash, but Mia and I are fine, and I can look after you both. There is enough of me to go around."

"I don't need to be looked after," I said, feeling defensive.

I had no clue what Levi was up to with this. I knew how he'd reacted after the announcement of our engagement had gone out. How he'd told my brother never to breathe my name to him again. Those words had hurt. I was probably never supposed to hear them, but still I had.

"I never said you needed looking after. I said, if you want to date someone, why not date me?"

I met his eyes, and in those few seconds that we stood there looking at one another, not a single reason came to my mind why I shouldn't date him. I should have had a thousand reasons, but I never even had a good reason for leaving him the first time. It wasn't because he'd just had a baby dropped in his lap from some woman in one of his earlier relationships. It wasn't because he'd had a one-night stand with her while he'd promised me a future with him. I knew our arrangement. He'd always been clear on his wants and promises. My reason wasn't because of anything other than being afraid to help him with Mia, because the thought of stepping up and being a mother at such a young age absolutely terrified me. I did not know how to take care of myself, never mind someone else. So, I chose myself and I walked away from something that could have been great because I'd been too unsure of myself.

"Well? What is your reason?" he said, taking a step closer to me from which I stepped away.

He stood there, waiting for me to come up with something, but I had nothing, and the more I looked into his eyes, the further from nothing I got.

"You don't have a reason, do you?" he questioned, a tiny smirk coming to his lips.

"Don't you have errands to run?" I asked, trying to change the subject.

"Answer my question first, Scarlett. Errands can wait. I have a few hours."

"What about practice?" I muttered.

"Day off," he said, his stare growing more intense.

I stood there, staring into his eyes, growing more frustrated with myself by the second.

"Alright then, no reasons" he said, clapping his hands together. "I guess that means you should prepare yourself."

"For what?"

"Our date this coming Saturday night."

I was pretty sure there was shock written all over my face as he moved closer to me.

"Saturday?" I murmured, swallowing hard.

"Yes, Saturday, say seven. I'll pick you up here and we'll head out for the evening. We won't be super late, but make sure you at least bring something warm to wear. It's supposed to be a little on the cooler side that evening.

"What…. What about Mia?" I muttered, praying that he'd come to his senses and realize he still had a little girl at home.

"What about her? She has a nanny, and I already know she is available that night because I made sure of it before I came down here."

"You what?" I asked.

"Scarlett, you should know me better than this. I

always have a plan when I'm going to make a play, on the ice and off."

"Levi, if you think I'm just going to drop everything and start seeing you only—"

He smirked.

"What's there to smirk about?" I questioned.

"I didn't think you were just going to roll over and go out with me, Scarlett. Oh, and I said nothing about being exclusive."

"You just said that you always make a plan before making a play. How was I supposed to take it?" I questioned.

He looked at me and shrugged his shoulders. "Take it how you want. I'm just trying to make up for my behavior from last night, and I figured treating you to a night out was a good way to do it."

"Is that so?

"Yep, plus, sometimes I get a challenge of having to work for something." He winked.

"Work for what?" I asked as he walked over and pressed a kiss to my cheek, the scent of his cologne invading my nose.

"I hope you have a good day, and just a reminder, you probably shouldn't leave that yogurt too much longer in the sun. I would hate to see you get sick from eating it."

He pulled me against him, smiled as he let me go,

and made his way back toward the door. I stood there, not knowing what to do or say. Part of me wanted to stop him, ask him if he was feeling alright.

"Oh, Scarlett, you should probably keep an eye out for some surprises this week. Never know when I might be in the mood to add a few gifts to make you forgive me a little quicker."

I was about to respond when I heard the door shut.

I stood there, looking at the closed door, completely shocked. What the hell just happened?

Chapter 6

Levi

I stood on the ice, my chin resting on the top of my stick as we all listened to Dylan's plan of attack for tonight's game. We broke our team talk when Coach Thompkins returned and called Dylan over for a quick one-on-one. As we waited for Dylan to return, I skated around the guys as they talked.

"What's everyone up to this weekend?" Lucas asked, shooting a puck my way, which I shot down toward the net, lifting my arms in victory as it went in.

"Peyton wants to go shopping for baby clothes. That's where I'll be," Clay said.

"We've been invited to have dinner with Dylan and Aurora. No, wait, actualy, we are referees is more like it. Dinner with her mom and Dylan's dad. Should be a good time," Knox said, rolling his eyes.

"Lucky you." Lucas chuckled. "What about you, Colton."

"New furniture is being delivered to my new place. Then I guess I'll be working on unpacking. Did you want to help, Levi?" he questioned. "You can bring Mia. Just bring some of her toys."

"Can't," I added.

"What do you mean? What the hell do you have going on that you can't help me out?"

I wasn't sure I wanted to divulge too much information to the guys right now.

"I have a date," I answered, keeping my head down.

"A date? With who?" Lucas asked. "Do we know her?"

There was no way I was going to mention Scarlett's name yet. So, I shook my head. "Just a girl from my building. Nothing serious."

It wasn't unlike me to have the occasional date. I'd dated most nights this past summer before Mia had returned from her grandparents to live with me. She'd been rather a surprise to the guys too, since I'd not mentioned her to them when I first came to the team, but they'd welcomed her with open arms, especially Colton

"Wow, so you even date when you have the little peanut at home?" Colton questioned. "What if you guys want to…oh, I don't know…return to your place and take a roll in the sheets?"

I rolled my eyes and shook my head. What did he think went on in my world, what with a nearly seven-year-old sleeping in the bedroom next to mine? I was lucky if I had enough time to watch some porn and get myself off without Mia bursting into my room on me. It most definitely wasn't his apartment. The guy always had women coming and going.

"Well, when that happens, I use your place," I said, chuckling as his eyes widened. "Usually when you're still out of a town after a game."

"Fuck you." He chuckled, punching me in the arm as I skated past him.

I STRETCHED before I walked out of the treatment room. Physio the day after game night always felt amazing, until today.

"Feeling better?" Lorelai questioned as she made

some notes in my file, like she always did after my appointments.

"Much, at least until everything stiffens up again." I chuckled.

I'd been hit hard against the boards one-night last week, during the second period, and while I'd not hurt myself, I'd been struggling with some lower back pain. I'd been told to check in with Aurora since she was the one on staff at the game that night, but I'd refused, claiming things were fine.

"I'm sure. It's not a wonder your back is killing you. Your glutes, hams, and quads were super tight, even your calves. You've been stretching after practices and games, haven't you?" she questioned, looking at me.

"Of course." I lied, avoiding her eyes.

"Levi…."

"Fine, I have been but probably not as much as I should be." I shrugged. "However, that hit I took last night didn't help either."

"You think?" She giggled. "You should have been in here last week."

She was right and I knew it. Truth was, I hadn't been stretching at all, and I was now paying for it. She and I had talked about this, and I knew it was impor-tant, but I'd been racing to get off the ice and, on my way, back home most of this past week, especially with Mia not feeling well. I hated burdening Mrs. Fletcher with a sick and crying child, even when she assured me many times that it was alright.

"Levi, make sure you take the extra time, even if you do it at home. I know you take off quickly because of Mia, so I understand. Let's get you scheduled for next week, before the away games, okay? We need to get those muscles loosened to prevent an injury that could take you out for part, if not for the rest, of the season."

"Okay," I answered.

"We'll do it during your practices. That way Mia is still here in the building with the daycare team. Heck she can even come down here while you are in treatment if it makes you feel better. Now you travel what, Tuesday through Friday?" she asked, looking over her schedule.

"Wednesday to Friday," I answered, checking my schedule on my phone.

"Yep, I had the wrong week. Okay, how about Monday and Tuesday, after practice."

"See you then," I said, adding the appointments to my calendar.

I FINALLY GOT Mia down for the night, showered, and had just sat down to relax and watch some TV when my phone started pinging with messages. Yawning, I leaned forward and grabbed my phone to see a string of messages from the guys. Frowning, I opened it up, wondering which one of us was going through a crisis and needed help.

Colton: Breaking News: Anderson has a date with some hot chick!

Dylan: Congrats Levi, who's the lucky lady?

Knox: Shouldn't we be saying unlucky? I mean, look at him?

Dylan: No, lucky...don't be a dick.

Clay: Well, he has that way about him. He comes by it honestly. I mean, at least that is what his sister says.

Knox: Not this again...

Clay: You started it. Besides, you should want the best outcome for your teammates, me included.

Lucas: Exactly Clay, I agree, I don't see that here.

Knox: Kill it Lucas, and Clay, I've always wanted the best for my teammates, until one of them went behind my back and did my little sister.

Clay: Seriously?? Are we still on this???

Knox: We'll be on that forever.

Dylan: Alright you two, let's be nice and get back to being friends, and let us get back to the matter that has been brought to our attention. Anderson, who's the lucky woman?

God, did these guys not know how to behave themselves? I let out a sigh and began typing. How had I become the one who was in a crisis?

Levi: It's nothing really, just a little dinner date.

Colton: Dinner or sex?

Lucas: Is that all you think about?

Colton: What food? Don't you think about food?

Lucas: Really? Food? You think we don't know you? Haha

Colton: That's right. I think about food all the time. You all should know that.

Levi: He's right, he has a bigger appetite than Knox

Knox: Says who? My sexual appetite is pretty large.

Colton: Not as large as mine.

Knox: Care to put that to a test?

Dylan: WHOA….ANYWAY…where are you taking the lucky lady?

Levi: I was thinking of taking her to The Orchid Lounge

Dylan: Oh, that new Japanese place? Supposed to be excellent.

Knox: Let's not tell Aurora or Lorelai that, I know Lorelai has been hinting to me that they both want to go.

Dylan: Same here, Aurora hasn't given up yet, she left one of their menus on the dining room table tonight.

Knox: Levi, please come back with some horrible reviews.

Colton: Shit, this girl can't just be any girl if you're taking her there. Have you seen the prices? It's fucking expensive as shit!

Levi: It's not that bad.

Colton: For a first date it is…jesus, how about you date me then? I'll even put out on the first date!

Levi: *eye roll* I saw the prices, and I'm not interested in your offer, thanks Colton.

I thought for a second. Did I make a mistake by telling them where I was planning on taking Scarlett? Was the cost of the meal really too much for a first date scenario?

Clay: *whistles, cough cough* You must really like this girl a lot….

Levi: Why do you say that?

Clay: I don't know. I wouldn't take a first date to a place like that…

Knox: Are you telling me you wouldn't take Peyton there?

Clay: Not what I said.

Dylan: While I'd agree with you on that Clay, maybe Levi is trying to impress the girl and just doesn't want to tell us. He is entitled to his privacy as well.

Levi: Thanks, Dylan

Dylan: No problem

Lucas: I don't know. Maybe something else is going on and he's been hiding her from us.

Levi: Okay, then where would you guys suggest going?

I grabbed my water and took a drink while I waited, and those three little dots bounced around. These guys were ridiculous, as if the place I'd been planning on taking Scarlett was too over-the-top for a first date. In my mind, nothing would ever be too over-the-top for Scarlett.

Colton: I don't know. Maybe cook the girl dinner at your apartment for a first date. That is what I would do.

Clay: Even if you want to impress her?

Colton: What's that supposed to mean?

Dylan: I've seen your cooking, let's just say that was a fair question.

Colton: I'll bring you lunch or dinner next week. May not look great, but the shit I cook takes fucking amazing.

Dylan: I'll take your word for it.

Levi: Look, I'm gonna go relax, I'm open to suggestions when you guys have any...

Knox: What about The Lighthouse?

Levi: She's allergic to seafood

Dylan: What about The Sunset?

Levi: Okay, I'll entertain that one.

Clay: I'm sure wherever you decide to take her she'll love it.

Lucas: I'm with Colton. Make her dinner. Or better yet, hire Colton to make dinner for the pair of you.

Colton: I'm not a chef...

Dylan: we know ;)

Knox: Yes, we know that.

Colton: Kill it...lol

Levi: I could make her dinner, but Mia...

Lucas: Shit, I forgot about the little one...

Colton: Plus, he can't just take her back to his bedroom after dinner with that little peanut running around.

Levi: My god, guys, it's a first date... jesus...what do you think I am?

Colton: stopped no one before...a little wine...a little candlelight, soft music and the girls melting in the palm of your hand...or better yet, you're melting in the palm of hers.

Dylan: That could be true, if she isn't throwing up after she ate what you cooked, haha

Knox: Sure is, all that romantic stuff gets Lorelai every time...

Levi: I've got to go, Mia is up.

Dylan: Later, let us know what you decide. We'll lend a hand with other suggestions.

Knox: Enjoy your night with your little lady. I know I'm going to enjoy mine.

Lucas: We'll drop more ideas as we think of them

Clay: You can count on us.

Levi: Why am I'm suddenly worried about that?

I smiled as I dropped the phone down on the table, got up from where I was sitting, and went to see what Mia needed.

Chapter 7

Scarlett

I'd just finished my article on the last two Dominators away games and sat back in my chair, grabbing my mug of hot coffee. I took a sip while I read over my article. I placed my mug back on the table, just as my stomach let out a loud, displeased growl. I had been so busy today that I'd had nothing to eat since breakfast. I'd planned to make something to eat when I'd got home, but that had slipped my mind when I thought about my upcoming date with Levi on Saturday night. This week had flown by, making the night of our date come much faster than I was prepared for.

I got up from my chair and began searching through the fridge as my stomach let out another growl. I'd meant to stop on my way home and get some groceries but wanted to get my article done for tomorrow's deadline.

I huffed, grabbed a slice of bread from the bag, and then opened the cupboard to grab the peanut butter, only to find that the jar was empty. I leaned up against the counter and ripped a piece off the slice of bread, shoving it into my mouth, debating what to order for dinner. I finished the slice and was about to grab another when someone knocked on the door.

I wasn't expecting anyone.

I pulled the door open, and there stood a delivery man holding a bag of food. My mouth watered at the smell of what I was certain was Penang.

"For you, Miss," he said, holding the bag out for me to take.

"I'm sorry, but I think you have the wrong unit," I said, going to close the door before I tore the bag from his hands.

He placed his hand on the door, holding it open, and glanced down at the receipt and shook his head. "Nope, Unit 1310," he said, pointing to the number outside my unit.

"Oh well, someone must have written the unit down wrong, because I ordered nothing," I said, shrugging my shoulders, once again moving to shut the door.

"Miss, I'm sorry, but I have an order here for you, from Bangkok Thai. One order of fresh vegetable rolls, one order of chicken Penang, and one order of medium chicken pad Thai, no shrimp because of an allergy."

I frowned. That would have been exactly what I'd ordered, and there were only two people who would have known my exact order, Scottie and Levi.

"Okay, well, what do I owe you?" I said, feeling confused but desperate now as the scent of the food hit me, causing my stomach to grumble and cramp.

"No charge. The bill has been taken care of," he said, smiling as he held the bag out for me to take.

Confused as hell, I took the bag and was about to shut the door when I stepped back out into the hall to see the delivery driver waiting for the elevator.

"Excuse me, but do you know who placed the order?" I questioned.

"I'm sorry, I don't. I just drive and deliver. If you want to know who ordered it, just call the restaurant and ask," he said, smiling.

I nodded. "Thank you."

I shut and locked the door and carried the bag into the kitchen, the smell of food making me feel nauseous as my stomach ached in anticipation of being filled. I reached into the bag and dove straight for the spring rolls, taking a bite, while I pulled the other two containers from the bag. While separating the containers, I found a folded piece of paper between them and opened it.

Hope this wasn't too much. Thought I'd surprise you after a long week. Enjoy. Levi.

Of course, it was Levi. Scottie would have ordered it but left me with the bill. I knew my brother too well, I thought as I crumpled the note and continued loading food onto my plate.

Once I'd eaten, I showered, watched a little TV, and then crawled into my bed. I'd just gotten comfortable and grabbed my phone, opening the message thread between Levi and me. I tapped the edge of my phone, debating what to send. Did I want to keep this lighthearted, or did I want to be serious? Did I want to thank him or give him shit? I had no idea why he would have done this. Regardless, I had no clue how to start the conversation. I glanced at the clock. He probably wasn't even back in his hotel room yet. It was only a little past ten.

I began typing a message, then paused and deleted it. On the second try, I typed out a simple thank you for dinner, then deleted it, then retyped it and hit send, and then placed my phone down on the bed, picking up the book I was reading.

I'd just gotten into the chapter when my phone vibrated. Reaching for it, I saw Levi had responded.

Levi: Glad you enjoyed.

I smiled as I read his words, then stopped myself.

Scarlett: I did, thank you, I was starving.

Levi: Glad it did the job then.

Scarlett: It did, but I'm confused. How did you remember what my exact order was from pretty much any Thai restaurant?

Levi: I remember lots of things. Plus, I used to send that order to you when you were studying for your exams every year when you were in school. It was the only thing you'd eat. Hard to forget something you did many times a year for five straight years.

I softly smiled as I stared at his words on my screen. He was right. He had always ordered that for me, especially when I was in the middle of writing a paper or studying for an exam. It was my comfort food and basically the only thing I could eat when stressed.

Scarlett: I remember. Though, I'll admit, it scares me you remember.

Levi: Why?

Scarlett: Most people can barely get their own orders right, and it has been years since you ordered food for me.

Levi: It hasn't been that long.

Scarlett: Been long enough.

Levi: Do you still remember what I like to eat on pizza?

Scarlett: How could I forget pineapple and anchovies, enough to make someone gag...

Levi: ...and it's been how long since we shared a pizza?

I see what you are doing here, Levi.

Levi: uh huh, no comeback, exactly what I thought.

> Scarlett: I'm confused. A few days ago you acted like you hated me, and in the past week you somehow agreed to get me to go out with you on a date, and you've ordered me dinner. Why are you doing all this? Did Scottie put you up to it?

I waited while the three dots bounced around, then stopped. I stared at the screen, wondering why he'd stopped typing. Then, figuring he must be with the guys in the locker room. I was just about to shut my phone off when his name popped up.

> Levi: I wanted to, and no one put me up to anything. I told you; I wanted to make it up to you for being an ass.

> Scarlett: I see. So, you say you remember things. What else do you remember that I might have forgotten?

Once again, I watched those three little dots bounce around, waiting for a response, then they stopped and started again, then stopped and started one last time.

> Levi: Would you like to talk on the phone?

Suddenly, I felt hot and sweaty as I stared at his question. I swallowed hard, my hands shaking. We hadn't talked on the phone since I'd been away at school. I didn't know why I felt so nervous. I talked on the phone all the time at work. This was no different. I could just pretend I was interviewing him, something I did often.

Levi: Well? Time's ticking....

Scarlett: Aren't you with the team?

Levi: Is that no?

What was wrong with me? My skin was clammy; my heart was racing. This was ridiculous, I thought to myself as I took a deep breath. Was I still hung up on him?

I opened my browser and pulled up his sports profile and looked at some pictures of him that were attached. After looking at a dozen photos of him, I minimized the screen and moved back to our conversation.

Scarlett: No, I just figured you'd still be with them. The game barely ended an hour and a half ago.

I'd just sent that message and my phone rang, causing me to jump. I looked at the screen and saw his name there as my ringtone played. The same ringtone

I'd saved on my phone specifically for him. I swallowed hard. I could hear my heart racing in my ears as I answered the call.

My voice shook as I answered. "Hello."

"Expecting someone else, or hoping for someone else?" His deep voice poured over the phone, followed by a chuckle.

"No. I'm just surprised you called me instead of messaging me back through messenger first. How did you know my number was the same?" I asked, settling under the covers.

"Lucky guess? I'm glad you enjoyed dinner."

"I did, thank you. It was a pleasant surprise."

"Well, I figured since I was ordering for Mia and her nanny that I'd order you a little something as well."

"Ah, I see?" I asked, giggling.

"To be honest, I was hoping to prove that you aren't making a mistake by going out with me on Saturday night. I know you were hesitant, and probably would have declined, had I not of walked out the door on you," he said, his voice lowering.

I stared at the ceiling and closed my eyes, letting out the breath I was holding. How I'd forgotten what this man could be like. That deep, sexy voice I used to love listening to after a long day. Most nights when I first moved away from home, it was the only thing that brought me comfort. It had also brought me to orgasm time and time again, listening to him talk dirty to me over the phone. I could still remember the first time we'd had phone sex, how turned on I got listening to him.

I kicked the covers off me, trying to cool myself off. I'd never realized how many things I'd just shoved to the back of my mind after I'd ended things with him. I guess it was easier than remembering the things he'd done for me and with me over the years.

"You were never a mistake, Levi," I whispered, closing my eyes, knowing he'd probably already heard the vulnerability in my voice.

"I wasn't?"

"No, you weren't. I was the one who made the…."

I stopped speaking. There was no way I could divulge this to him, and I shouldn't.

"You were the one who what?" he questioned, then went silent, waiting for me to respond.

"Levi, you know, I think I'm going to say good night. It's late and we both have work in the morning," I said, suddenly feeling a way more vulnerable than I ever intended to get with him on this call.

"See you Saturday then."

"See you then."

"Night, Scarlett."

"Night, Levi."

Chapter 8

Levi

I lay in bed with my hands behind my head. The sun was just coming up. Mia slept soundly against me. I rolled onto my side, careful not to move the bed too much for fear I might wake her.

I'd gotten home late last night, and once Mrs. Fletcher left, Mia woke from a bad dream. Since I didn't feel like spending the night on the couch after being away from home, I'd grabbed her stuffed bear and favorite blanket and brought her into bed with me.

I closed my eyes, hoping I'd be able to get another half hour of sleep before Mia woke, but my mind wouldn't shut off.

I rolled over, this time sitting up on the edge of the bed and running my hands through my hair. I'd been like this since the other night, unable to concentrate and sleep, right after the call with Scarlett.

I grabbed my phone and scrolled through my photo albums, finally coming to the one I'd made for our photos. I'd kept every single photograph we'd taken together over the years, and I looked through them as I sat there.

God, as much as I never wanted to admit it to myself, I still held feelings for her. The moment I'd heard her say that I hadn't been a mistake, I felt a trickle of relief. As much as I'd told her brother I didn't want to know things about her, it hadn't been the truth at all; it had been something I'd had to do to protect myself.

I ran my hands through my hair again as I flipped through the photos of us. Tonight, I'd be taking Scarlett out for this date and the more I thought about it, the more I felt ill. I was so nervous.

Things between us ended so abruptly, before they even got started, and I'm being honest when I say that I felt jilted. Then, while I was still trying to figure out how to win her back, Duncan swung in and took her right out from under me. Some would say that he didn't steal her from me, but I begged to differ.

I was so busy trying to get things under control with Mia and my job, the next thing I knew, I'd gotten a call from Scottie, telling me I'd better not fuck around or I'd risk losing her to Duncan. I didn't listen, mainly because I never thought that would happen, and then next thing I knew, a year had flown by, and I was staring at an engagement announcement.

I'd never forget that moment, opening up the paper and seeing it. In a moment it felt as if all the air had left the apartment. My throat was tight, and my chest hurt, and suddenly the feeling I'd never gotten a fair shot with her crept up and has sat with me ever since. Perhaps that was what the problem was right now. Even though I had told her this was just two single people heading out on a date, I was afraid I'd actually blow the one and only second chance I'd probably ever have with her, and somewhere deep inside of me, even if I didn't want to admit it, I wanted that second chance.

I closed the folder of images down and took a deep breath, letting it out slowly, trying my best to calm down, when I felt the bed move. I looked over my shoulder to see Mia lift her head, open her eyes, then roll over and fall back to sleep.

I went back and checked my email, happy to see that the confirmation for tonight's reservation at The

Orchid Lounge had just come in. Then I worried that perhaps the guys were right, maybe this place was a tad over-the-top. Perhaps I should just cancel and just make her dinner here. Mia could go down and stay with Mrs. Fletcher instead.

Placing my phone back on the charger, I got up and headed into the bathroom, turned on the shower, then quickly checked to see Mia was still sleeping right in the centre of my king-sized bed. Certain she wouldn't fall out, I jumped into the shower quickly, shaved and got dressed, then made my way out of the bathroom to find Mia sitting in the middle of the bed, rubbing her tired eyes, while holding Potato, her favorite stuffed pig.

"Morning," I said, going over to her and lifting her up.

"Morning, Daddy," she mumbled, resting her head on my shoulder.

"Are you hungry?" I asked, kissing her forehead.

She nodded, rubbing her eyes again as I carried her into the kitchen and sat her in her chair at the breakfast bar.

"What would you like?" I questioned.

"Oatmeal and cimonin," she said, reaching for her crayons and colouring book.

"Oatmeal and cinnamon it is," I said, moving

around the kitchen. "Want some blueberries?" I asked, pulling out the container.

She nodded her head. "What are we doing today?" she asked, taking a blueberry from the container.

"Well, we are going to do a little shopping."

"What for?" she questioned. "Ohhh could we go to the toy store?"

I couldn't help but chuckle. "Yes we can, and I need to get some flowers," I said, dumping a little more oatmeal into the pot and stirring it as it cooked.

"What for?"

"For a lady," I answered, turning to look over at her, hoping to gage her reaction.

She looked up at me and smiled. "Daddy, are they for me?"

"No, sweet pea, not for you."

"Oh. But Mrs. Fletcher says I'm a little lady. Especially when I wear my pink dress."

"Yes, that is true, but they aren't for you. If you'd like some, I'll get you some as well, but these are for another lady."

"Who?" she asked, looking up at me with large innocent eyes.

I only ever dated when she was with my parents. I'd decided a while ago that I needed to protect her from the hurt if things didn't work out between me and whomever I was seeing, and I'd just found it easier to stay single until she was older.

"Do you remember Scarlett?" I asked.

She shook her head as she chose another crayon.

"The lady we were talking to our front of our building?"

"Oh, the lady who dropped coffee on my head?"

I couldn't help but smile at how she remembered things.

"That would be the one."

"You're buying her flowers because she dropped coffee on my head?" she questioned, her face scrunched up in curiosity.

"No, silly. Now, put your crayons away and eat up," I said, placing the bowl of hot oatmeal in front of her before sitting down beside her with my bowl. "Just make sure you blow on it, it's hot."

"But, Daddy, why are you buying her flowers?"

"Because she is my friend."

Mia looked up at me and nodded, then smiled. "Can we get her pink flowers?"

I smiled to myself as I took the first mouthful of oatmeal, then added a handful of blueberries.

"We can, now eat up."

"I will. I want to finish my picture first," she said, humming away to herself as she continued to color.

"OKAY, Levi, what time will you be home tonight?" Mrs. Fletcher asked as I shoved the last of the food into the fridge that I'd grabbed at the grocery store.

"I won't be too late. Probably ten, but if you're tired, please crash in the spare room."

"No worries, Levi. Ten isn't too late. I hope you enjoy yourself."

"Thanks, you guys have a good night. Pizza should be here shortly," I said, winking at Mrs. Fletcher and grabbing my keys and wallet from the counter.

"Levi, I told you I'd make dinner."

"I know, but you already do so much for us."

"Daddy…don't forget the flowers," Mia said, running over to where we were standing, carrying the bouquet.

I bent down and took them from her and kissed her on the cheek. "You be a good girl tonight and do as you're told."

"I will," she said, taking off for the living room where she was watching cartoons and playing with the new toy I'd gotten for her.

I made my way down to the thirteenth floor and knocked on the door. Finally, I heard a movement on the other side and was greeted with a smile when the door opened.

"Hey." I smiled, shoving my one hand in my pocket and holding out the flowers for her to take. "These are for you."

She smiled and took the bouquet of light-lavender and pink-colored carnations mixed with baby's breath.

"Mia helped me pick them out. She insisted you needed some pink." I chuckled.

Scarlett smiled. "What does that mean? I need some pink?"

I shrugged. "I haven't got a clue. She calls you the lady who dumped coffee on her head, so maybe it has something to do with the colorful shade your cheeks turned that day." I winked.

"Well, let me put these in a vase, and then we'll get going. Where are we off to?"

"You'll see." I winked as she placed the flowers in some water and then grabbed her jacket.

We made our way down to the parking lot and over to my car, where I opened the door for her and waited for her to get in.

"Levi, I can open a door."

"I know you can. Just trying to be a gentleman."

I PULLED into the parking spot in front of The Orchid Lounge and glanced over to see Scarlett looking over at me, smiling.

"Wait here," I said, climbing out of the driver's seat while leaving the car running. I made my way into the restaurant and then returned ten minutes later with a bag of food, which I placed in the back seat.

"Uh, Levi, what are we doing?" she questioned.

"Well, it was going to be a surprise, but I decided I didn't want to have dinner surrounded by many people, so I did the next best thing. We are having a private picnic over along the waterfront. That was why I reminded you to wear something warm."

She softly smiled as I backed out of the parking spot and headed toward the waterfront where I parked the car, shut off the engine, and climbed out. I opened the trunk and grabbed two large blankets and the basket of things I'd packed and handed them to her while grabbing the food from the back seat.

We made our way over to an open area where we quickly threw one blanket down on the ground, then both sat down. She started pulling out plates and uten-sils from the basket, while I opened the chilled bottle of wine and poured each of us a glass. Then I dove into the bag of food and placed the containers on the ground.

After we'd eaten and we'd cleaned up, I poured some more wine into our glasses and leaned back on the blanket as we looked out over the water. Scarlett had grown quiet in the last little while. She'd been talking nonstop while we ate, but now, radio silence and I wondered what was on her mind.

"Care to tell me what you're thinking?" I asked.

She looked out over the water, thinking, weighing her words carefully like she used to when we first hung out, then shrugged.

"I don't know. It scares me how easy this is with you again."

I nodded, knowing exactly what she meant. I'd felt it too; it seemed like no time had passed and that we'd never been apart. "I get that."

"It's like the other night when we were on the phone. Even before that, when we were texting. All this time had passed between us, and yet here we were, the same two people."

"But yet, we aren't the same two people."

"I know." She said, a far off look in her eyes."

"Does that scare you?"

"A little. Honestly, I thought you hated me."

I didn't want to look at her for fear she saw the

exact opposite in my eyes. I could never hate her. I figured that out for myself this morning when going back through our old photos.

"Why would you think that?"

"How could I not? You haven't exactly been warm to me since I got here. Plus, I know you told Scottie you wanted to know nothing more about me."

I fidgeted with the blanket as I watched a boat in the water.

"Scarlett, I have never hated you. How the hell could I. I was in love with you, and you were the only person I could see myself spending the rest of my life with. Honestly, I did that because I had to protect myself and shoving you out of my life was the way I had to do it."

"So why were you so cold to me the day I spilled my coffee?"

I couldn't help but chuckle.

"What's so funny?"

"Well, let's see, I really was late, tugging around a six-year-old who has zero concept of time. It isn't always easy with her, then for that to happen, I guess I just lost my temper. It had already been a trying day. Plus, to be honest, I felt frazzled. You were the last person in the world I'd ever have expected to come to Vancouver, then to top that off, to move into my building, nonetheless. I guess I was in some kind of shock."

"That makes sense." She smiled, then glanced at me, her eyes immediately returning to the water.

I reached over and grabbed her hand, gently taking it in mine. "I never hated you. You broke my heart, and I still never hated you."

"I don't think I broke your heart, Levi." She started laughing as she turned to look at me.

"You don't?"

"No, I don't. We never really were anything to one another aside from friends."

I watched as her eyes started to glaze over and she quickly wiped at them, then looked away from me. If she truly thought that she was going to be in for a surprise, because I'd always looked at her as more than that.

"Well, this guy here begs to differ. Do you remember the weekend you stayed with me right after graduation, the same weekend Mia arrived?"

She nodded her head and met my eyes.

"That weekend, you were going to see your mom and dad. Scottie was coming out for guys' weekend. Remember?"

"Yes, my parents were so mad that he would not be around to celebrate my graduation that they actually gave him shit."

"Well, he wasn't coming out for guys' weekend. He was coming to go with me to pick out an engagement ring. I'd planned on proposing the night you officially moved in."

"What?" she asked, the words barely audible as she looked at me. "We'd never even slept together; we'd never even really dated, aside from that one month."

"So what? I already knew in my heart you were the one I wanted to be with, and to be honest, I wanted to wait for our wedding night, before we slept together."

"You're fucking with me," she said, a smile on her face, ready to burst into laughter.

"I'm not. Scottie came, my mom stayed with Mia, and we went out and I ordered the ring, figuring you'd be over everything by the time you returned from seeing your parents the following weekend. Either that or you'd at least be calm enough to sit down with me and have a conversation. I gave you the space you needed, excited to see you the following weekend, but you called me on the Friday night and announced you weren't coming back, then said your goodbyes."

She studied me. I could tell she wanted to say something, but to be honest, I didn't want her to say anything at all. She just had to know.

"Levi, I didn't know…"

"Of course you didn't know. How could you of? I'd have killed Scottie had he of said anything."

"Why didn't you stop me? Why didn't you fight for me?"

"Well, for starters, I knew you well enough to know that once you'd decided, nothing I'd have said would have changed anything. I could also tell because we'd barely spoken the entire week, and there hadn't been a single time since I'd known you that we'd even go twelve hours before messaging, emailing or speaking to one another."

"Yeah, but why didn't you tell me about the ring?"

"What was I going to say, Scarlett? Just come home. I want to marry you?"

"Something like that?"

"How romantic would that of been?"

"I wouldn't have cared."

I chuckled. "Yes, you would have. Believe me, you would have. I wanted to give you a proposal you'd remember forever. Instead, I moved on, life took over, I picked up, put my focus where it needed to be, just like you did."

I saw her flinch at the last part.

"What happened between you two?" I questioned, wanting to know the truth.

She sat there, took a deep breath, and then shook her head.

"That is a story for another time. It's been enough heavy talk for tonight."

I nodded, somewhere deep inside of me agreeing with her. I'd never planned to tell her about the ring;

however, somehow it had slipped out before I could stop myself.

"Fair enough," I said, catching her shiver, then bring her hands up and rub her forearms.

"You cold?"

She nodded.

I shifted and rolled onto my side, moving over, resting my elbow on the mound of blankets I'd been leaning on.

"What are you doing?" she questioned.

"Come on over, I'll keep you warm. Be just like old times."

She softly smiled, then shivered again as another gust of cool wind came off the water, then moved in closer.

She leaned back against the rolled-up comforter behind us and lay back, her body sheltered from the wind by my body and looked up at me.

It had been forever since we were this close, and the scent of her perfume enveloped me.

"I'm so sorry I hurt you," she whispered as she looked up at me.

I didn't even need to second-guess what she said, I could already see the genuine look of regret in her eyes. I could also see the want in her eyes and, without thinking, I lowered myself and pressed my lips against hers. I didn't need anyone to tell me that this wasn't right; I felt it deep in my soul. I wanted it, and so did she.

The moment I was about to pull away was the same moment she brought her hand to the back of my head and snaked her fingers into my hair, kissing me back.

Chapter 9

Scarlett

His kiss was like a bolt of electricity moving through my body. The second his lips touched mine, my body felt alive. I closed my eyes, concentrated on my breathing, and ran my fingers through his thick hair. In a moment, everything we'd been through had been erased and we were right back where we were supposed to be.

He broke the kiss, looked down at me, and pushed my hair from my face and cupped my cheek. I didn't want this night to end, even though our conversation only moments ago had been serious and I'd wanted to shy away. Most of the night had been full of laughs, just the way it used to be.

"We should probably get going," he said, smiling down at me, before leaning down and placing another kiss on my lips.

Disappointment flooded me, but he was probably right. I glanced at my watch, seeing it was close to ten.

"Yeah, I guess we should." I smiled, pulling myself away from him and sitting up. "Work comes early, especially for you."

"Not because of work. I promised the sitter I'd be back before ten."

I nodded, standing, and began folding the one blanket we'd been using as a pillow.

Levi was quiet as he stood too, first adjusting himself and then taking the other blanket and quickly folding it, then grabbing the basket and glasses. Minutes later, we'd packed up the car and were on our way back to the condo.

When the elevator opened at my floor, he didn't step out, instead he just wished me a good night with a kiss on the cheek and I made my way to my unit and headed inside.

Monday morning came faster than I'd expected. I walked into the office on Monday morning feeling like I was walking on air, until the receptionist approached me and told me Carol wanted to see me. Immediately, the air that was under me holding me up evaporated as I walked into Carol's office.

She sat behind her desk, her glasses perched on the end of her nose. The second I entered she looked up at me from her seat.

"I heard you wanted to see me?"

"I did. Close the door, take a seat."

I did as she asked and watched as she opened her top desk drawer and pulled out an envelope and placed it in the centre of the desk, then looked at me.

"What's that?" I questioned.

"That is an envelope containing two tickets to the next two away games held by the Dominators. You have an outgoing flight leaving tomorrow night, returning on Friday morning."

I nodded and went to reach for the envelope when she cleared her throat, which made me pause.

"Scarlett, I have been doing some digging."

"Okay."

"As stated, I want an interview with Levi, but what I want more is to find out some things about his past."

I quickly averted my gaze back to the envelope on the desk, praying she would not mention what I thought she was going to mention.

"What about his past?" I questioned, clearing my throat.

"I want to know about his daughter."

Alarm bells rang inside of me. I knew Levi was completely protective of Mia and that there would be no way he'd answer questions regarding her.

"He has a daughter?" I asked, trying hard to fake what I already knew.

"He does. Not only do I want an article on him, but I want the dirt on where this child came from. He isn't married, in fact that man has never even been seen in the public eye with a significant other. So, I want you to hunt down the mother of his child, get an interview with her, find out what the hell happened between them."

"What? Why would I do something like that? Isn't this article supposed to be a highlight on him? On his career and how good of a player he is."

"Are you saying you won't do it?"

I sat there, not really knowing how to respond.

"Scarlett? Is that what you are telling me? Are you refusing to do this?"

"No, but when you are supposed to be highlighting a man's career, this isn't the way to go about it. I feel like it's sabotaging."

"All we are doing here is showing the fans what this man is about. The inability to commit. If you want to look at it from a different angle, he was with the Predators for how long, then moved to the Dominators, and now there is talk that he may move to the Enforcers. See, inability to commit.”

I frowned. I’d heard no such thing about him being in talks with him leaving Vancouver, and I kept my ear close to the ground when it came to switches and moves with all players. In fact, he seemed happy and settled here.

“So, can I count on you to have the article to me in a month? I want it published for his one year with them.”

I reached for the envelope in the centre of the desk and shoved it into my bag without saying another word.

“I won’t ask you again. Can I count on you? If not, I’ll take the tickets back and I’ll send John.”

“You will get what you ask for,” I said, my voice low.

“Good, your flight leaves at five. Don’t be late.”

I looked over my shoulder at Carol before I walked out of her office and made my way down to mine. I closed my door and leaned up against it. Instantly I began second-guessing my decision to come here. What the hell had I gotten myself into??

MY FLIGHT GOT in late last night, and I'd crashed immediately. Now, I sat in the New York arena doing research while watching the team practice.

I was knee deep into finding out who this girl was that had brought Mia to Levi. The one good thing was that I had her name. It was a name I'd never forget, and without that I'd have been dead in the water.

Skylar Payne had been an intern in public relations for the New York team when Levi played for them. They'd shared a one-night stand while at an away game, and one year and five months later, she appeared on his doorstep, jobless, with Mia. She was no longer in that profession after being caught sleeping with another player on the same team by his wife. Looked like times were hard for her now, being forced out of the career she'd loved.

I was so buried in reading information about her I didn't hear anyone come up behind me until I heard Levi clearing his throat.

"Well, well, aren't you up early?" He chuckled.

I slammed my computer shut and turned to look up at him. He stood there, two coffees in his hands, smiling down at me.

"Hey," I answered back, turning around, praying he hadn't seen what I'd been reading.

"You were pretty lost in whatever you were looking

up," he said, sitting down beside me. "Trying to get some sort of scoop on a player or something?"

"Yeah, something like that. I get like that when I'm doing research," I said, shoving my laptop into my bag at my feet. "How was practice?"

"It was practice, same as usual, grueling and painful." He chuckled.

"Where's the rest of the team?"

"Gone for food." He smiled. "I saw you up here, so I thought I'd come and say hello. So, what are you researching?"

"You must be hungry," I said, completely ignoring his question.

"So must you. I don't recall you being this much of an early bird, and I know you never ate before nine in the morning at the earliest."

How the hell did he remember all this stuff? I barely remembered what I had for dinner last night, and here he remembered shit that happened years ago.

"Yeah, come to think of it, I'm starving."

"Good. Care to join me?" he questioned.

I nodded my head, zipped up my bag, threw it over my shoulder, and followed him out of the arena.

I SAT in my room eating potato chips, working on the start of an article to cover this weekend's game. I grabbed my phone and opened up a new chat between Levi and myself and sent him a message.

> Scarlett: Can I ask you something?

> Levi: What's up?

> Scarlett: Would you allow me to interview you?

> Levi: Why?

> Scarlett: Well, you told me if I asked, you'd allow it. I'd like to write an article on you.

Some days, I really hated those three little bouncing dots and today was one of those days. Then his message came through.

> Levi: We can talk about it. No promises. What are you doing?

I COULD TELL from his short answer that there was no point in talking about it now. He meant what he said and that was his way of closing off the conversation before it even got started.

Scarlett: Work.

Levi: It's late, you should be relaxing.

Scarlett: We never sleep.

Levi: We? Am I interrupting something?

Scarlett: No, we as in reporters. We never sleep, and just so you know, my room is empty.

Levi: You don't need to explain yourself to me. If you have company, you have company.

Scarlett: I'm not explaining myself to you.

Levi: I beg to differ.

Scarlett: You are impossible.

Levi: Nope, just don't want to interrupt something if it's going down.

> Scarlett: What makes you think I'd have messaged you and would continue chatting with you if, as you put it, something was going down?

> Levi: I don't know, maybe you're reconnecting with Duncan, and he kisses like a lizard.

I COULDN'T HELP but laugh out loud at his last comment.

> Scarlett: *rolls eyes*

> Levi: Just saying, maybe you needed an out. Am I your out, Scarlett?

> Scarlett: You aren't my out because I'm not in anything I need out of. There is no one here.

> Levi: So, you're not reconnecting with Duncan right now?

I STARED AT MY PHONE. How was I supposed to answer that? Levi knew something had happened between us, he just didn't know what it was, or how final it was. Was I just supposed to come out and say he'd passed away?

Levi: I knew it…if he's going down on you, tell me to go away.

I buried my face in my hands at his comment, my cheeks heating.

Scarlett: Not possible

Levi: Not possible? Sure, it is. He has a tongue, doesn't he? Oh wait, please tell me he knows how to pleasure you with his tongue?

Scarlett: This is a stupid conversation and I'm not continuing it on.

Levi: Really? Why is that? Because you're embarrassed by the fact he doesn't know how to pleasure you, or because you wish he was pleasuring you right now? Or perhaps you wish I were pleasuring you right now, because I will say I know how to use mine.

I WANTED TO SCREAM. I should have just told him the other night what had happened, and then we wouldn't be having this conversation.

Levi: Come on, the girl I used to know would have laughed at this.

> Scarlett: You are the one who said we are different people now. What if I'm not the same girl you used to know?

> Levi: Well, you did fit in my arms the same way and you still kiss like the girl I used to know ;)

I stared at his message. He said nothing that wasn't true.

> Scarlett: Levi, I have something I have to tell you.

> Levi: Shoot! I'm all ears….and you never know, maybe tongue ;)

> Scarlett: Duncan died last year.

The moment I hit send, I felt like a huge jerk. This wasn't the way to tell someone something like this. As I waited for him to respond, I sat there staring at the screen, feeling horrible. As time passed, there was —no return message, no bouncing dots, nothing—but still I sat there staring at my screen, waiting.

I put my phone down on my desk and placed my head in my hands. I'd always known that Levi had issues when Duncan and I had announced our engagement. Scottie had told me that, and he'd told me then that maybe it was time I should reconsider my relationship with him instead of tying myself to a guy I wasn't truly happy being with.

He wasn't wrong. I'd never been happy being with Duncan, and I'd told Scottie that frequently. While both Duncan and Levi were extremely committed to their work, Levi had this way of always making time for you, no matter what the circumstances.

When I was away at school and he was on the road, I could remember calling him after a long day. He'd be fifteen minutes from being on the ice and he'd still take the call. It never mattered to him. With Duncan, the only time he carved out for me was right before bed, or Sunday afternoons, and if there was an emergency while he was at work, I was on my own because he was totally off-limits.

I wiped the tears that were running down my cheeks and took a deep breath. I needed to pull myself together. I reached for a tissue when someone knocked on the door to my room. I glanced at the clock. It was a little late for it to be anyone from the hotel, I thought to myself, and since I was not expecting anyone, I was certain someone probably had the wrong room and would go away if I was quiet.

I wiped my eyes and nose and threw the tissue in the garbage, got up, and made my way over to bed when I heard another forceful knock. Letting out a breath, I made my way to the door and looked through the peephole. I couldn't see anything, which was weird. I turned the deadbolt, keeping the sliding bolt lock on, and opened the door to see Levi standing there. I quickly closed the door and removed the bolt lock, opening it up again.

"Levi? How did you know what room I was in?" I questioned, standing there, shocked that he'd found it.

"We know where all reporters stay," he said, his eyes washing over my face. "Can I come in?"

Of course, he already knew where I was staying. How could I forget their PR team would have handled not only the tickets but the booking of my room. I nodded. "Of course, you'd know where I was staying." I sniffled, averting my eyes from his.

He was looking at me. I could feel it, and I knew if I looked at him, there would be questions in his eyes that I'd have to answer. He'd take one look at me and know I'd been crying. He'd seen it a million times over the years. I didn't know what I was trying to hide from him, I just knew I didn't want to answer his questions.

"Can I come in?" he questioned again, his voice low.

I said nothing, simply stepped to the side and waited for him to enter, then closed the door.

"What did you want?" I asked, pushing past him and sitting down on the end of the bed.

"I'd never have made those remarks had I known about Duncan. I'm sorry."

"Don't worry about it." I sniffled. "It really doesn't matter."

"Yes, it does. I was being a jerk."

"It doesn't matter, Levi, seriously. He's gone. That part of my life is over."

"I never thought he'd have died. I figured that things just didn't work out between you. Regardless, I shouldn't have been that insensitive. After all, you were in love with him."

I stood up off the end of the bed and made my way over to the window, pulling the curtains back and looking out over the twinkling lights of the city. I could see Levi's reflection staring at me in the window.

"It's fine, Levi. Please. I know our relationship and engagement announcement hurt you, and I know how you protected yourself when those things happened," I said, looking out over the city, afraid to tell him the real reason I wasn't all that upset over his death.

I didn't need to focus on my reflection in the window to know he was right behind me. I could feel the heat from his body, that same familiar energy that spoke to my body in a way no one else's ever had. The moment he placed his hands on my arms, I crumbled. Heavy sobs racked my body. I fell back into his warmth and allowed it to envelop me as tears poured down my face.

"Hey, I got you," he whispered, placing a kiss on my temple. "I won't let you go, just let it all out," he said, as he wrapped his arms around me.

No, he had it all wrong. He thought I was crying because of Duncan.

"I can only imagine how you must feel, what you must be going through. Had I of known...well...I wouldn't have been such an insensitive jerk."

"It's not Duncan." I sniffled. "I...I don't think I ever..."

"That you ever what?"

"I never loved him."

There, I'd said it. The words had finally left my mouth, and the second they had I felt such a weight lift off me that I felt lightheaded.

"Sure, you did. You're probably going through one of those grief stages you hear people talk about. They pass. It's all part of the healing process," he whispered.

I pulled away from him. Scottie had been right. Sure, I grieved his loss, but I'd never truly loved Duncan, and it had taken me this long to realize it. It was a relationship I'd entered because I was mourning the loss of Levi, and at the time, anything was better than being alone. Scottie had told me that time and time again, told me to talk to Levi, to give myself grace, and give things time to settle, but I'd never listened. I knew better than anyone. Instead, I dove in headfirst, never stopping for one minute to think about what I was doing, and then I woke up one morning and found myself with a ring on my finger.

"It's not a stage of grief, Levi, at least not over the person you think it's over."

Levi looked at me, questions in his eyes. "Were you having an affair?" he asked. "It's okay if you were. I'd look at you no different."

"I wasn't having an affair, at least not one of the physical kind," I muttered.

"Oh, I get it, an emotional one. Those happen, and again, I don't look at you any different."

"It wasn't physical or emotional." I sighed, feeling frustrated.

"Okay then, you're going to have to spell it out to me because I'm lost."

"I was never in love with Duncan, Levi. I was never in love with him because I was still in love with you."

There, I'd said it. The words had flown out of my mouth before I could stop them. Levi stared at me. I could tell he didn't know what to say. After all these years, the truth finally came out.

Levi chuckled. Why he was laughing was beyond me because there was nothing funny about this situation at all.

"What's so funny?"

"Come on, Scarlett. You're fucking with me."

"Does it look like I'm fucking with you? I never got over you. Leaving was a mistake, Levi. I ran because I was scared. Ask Scottie if you don't believe me. He'll tell you."

Levi stood there looking at me, shock all over his face. I wanted him to say something, anything but he just stood there looking at me. Without a word, he turned, made his way to the door, and left the room. I waited there, waiting for him to knock, to come back, but there was nothing, he was gone.

Chapter 10

Levi

"What's with you this morning?" Dylan asked, coming to a stop in front of me.

I'd missed every single shot that had been sent my way in this morning's practice, and had even wiped out four times, which rarely happened during practice.

"I don't know. Guess I'm just not on my game." I sighed, not wanting to divulge the truth.

It wasn't every day you heard that the girl who ripped your heart out was still in love with you. Those words still shocked me, and it had been five days. Yes, five days since she uttered those words while we were in New York, and five days since I'd spoken to her after she'd said them. I'd avoided her at every turn and made it known because I certainly didn't know how to deal with any of it.

"Not on your game is right. God, I hope you don't play like that tomorrow night. We are on home turf. Can't disappoint the fans."

I nodded, taking one puck that was lying on the ice in front of me and shooting it toward the net, missing again.

"Here's hoping. Maybe I'll just sit this game out, tell the coach I fucked up my back or something."

Dylan gave me a worried look. "Levi, if you need to talk…"

"No, nothing is wrong. It's all good. Just having an off day." I sighed. "Or maybe an off week would be more accurate."

Once showered and changed, I headed up to find Mia at the daycare centre playing with one of the other player's kids. I waved from the door, and she immediately got up, put the things she was playing with away, and ran to me. Picking her up, I placed a kiss on her cheek, grabbed her jacket, and we made our way to the car.

Once Mia was in her car seat, I climbed into the driver's seat and immediately sent a text to Scottie. I don't know why, but I needed to know if what Scarlett had said was true. Sure, he'd tried to get me to work things out with her, but he'd said nothing that would have led me to believe she was unhappy.

Once I'd messaged, I pulled out of the spot and raced home.

MIA SLEPT SOUNDLY beside me in my bed. I glanced at the clock, letting out a yawn. It was only a little past two. She normally had a nap on practice day, and since she had been so tired when I had to get her up this morning, I wasn't in a rush to wake her from her nap just yet. In fact, I had just woken up. I adjusted the pillows behind me and grabbed my phone from my night table just in time to see Scottie's name flash on my screen.

Scottie: What's going on? How's the season going? I've been watching. You are on fire this year.

Levi: Thanks. It hasn't been too bad. How's things with you?

Scottie: Not bad, same as usual.

Levi: That's good.

Scottie: So, what's up? You said you
wanted to talk to me about something.

I looked at his question. Yes, that was what I'd said,
and I'd alluded to nothing more, probably as a way out
if I decided I didn't want to know the truth. I tapped
the edge of my phone, then began typing.

Levi: I wanted to talk to you about
Scarlett.

Scottie: Oh, is everything okay with
her? She hasn't messaged or called
me since before she left to watch your
game in New York. To be honest, I'm
getting a little worried.

Levi: So, she's ignoring you as well?

Scottie: What do you mean? Ignoring
me as well? What's going on out there?

Levi: After I treated her like shit, and
you wanted me to apologize, I took
her out on a date. Nothing serious
before you get all overprotective and
brotherly on me.

Scottie: She told me.

Levi: Of course she did.

Scottie: There isn't much she doesn't tell me.

I'd forgotten just how close they were, and just how much they shared with one another. So it somewhat shocked me to hear that she hadn't even spoken to him in the past few days.

Levi: Why didn't you tell me Duncan died?

Scottie: I didn't feel it was important information.

Levi: Not important information?

Scottie: Correct, how did you find out?

Levi: Scarlett told me, after I made an ass out of myself. When I went to apologize to her, she also told me she had never been in love with him. Did you know that?

There was no response. The phone went silent. The three little dots weren't bouncing, but I never took my eyes off the screen, because his silence only meant one thing.

Levi: did you know she was still in love with me, probably never fell out of love with me?

Scottie: Bro...

Levi: Don't hide it, did you know?

Scottie: I tried to tell you.

Levi: No, you didn't. You told me I should try to get her back.

Scottie: That's right and when I called you the night she got engaged, I was going to tell you she was still in love with you, but...

Levi: but I told you I didn't want to hear her name again.

Scottie: Precisely.

As I stared at my phone screen, the same feelings from the other night flooded me. Shock, confusion, and then anger. It was then Mia stirred. A crying child was something I really didn't need right at this moment, so I placed my hand on her back, letting her know I was here.

Scottie: Are you okay?

Levi: I've got to go, Mia is stirring.

Scottie: If you need to talk message, okay?

Levi: I think right now I just need to be alone.

I put my phone back down on the nightstand and then scooted down beside Mia, pulling her against me, hoping to comfort her enough that she would fall back to sleep.

AN HOUR LATER, Mia sat in the cart playing a game on my phone while I wandered the grocery store, filling the cart with things for this week. I just rounded a corner and banged right into another cart.

"I'm so sorry," I said, looking up to see Scarlett standing in front of me, looking disgruntled, until her eyes met mine.

"No, I'm sorry. I wasn't paying attention," she murmured, then averted her eyes from mine, bending over and grabbing a bag of cookies.

I glanced down at the few things she had in her cart and back at her. "Grocery shopping?" I questioned.

"Dinner," she muttered.

I glanced back at the items that lay on the bottom of her cart. She had a bag of popcorn, a bottle of soda, some cut-up mango, and now a bag of cookies.

"Dinner? Please tell me you're going to eat more than that?"

She looked at me and shrugged her shoulders. "I'm not all that hungry."

It was then Mia looked over her shoulder at Scarlett and smiled. "Hi," she said, grinning from ear to ear.

"Hi," Scarlett said back, smiling at Mia, but that smile didn't meet her eyes.

Mia turned back to me, held her little hand by her mouth, and asked, "Is she going to dump coffee on us again?"

I couldn't help but laugh at the look on Mia's face.

"It was fun!" She giggled, which caused Scarlett and me to laugh.

"Mia, this is my friend Scarlett," I said, looking over at her as she turned her attention to Mia.

"Daddy, she's pretty," Mia said, holding her small hand up in a wave.

"Yes, she is beautiful," I whispered back to Mia, then up to Scarlett as her eyes fell to mine.

"Levi, about last week…" Scarlett began, but I stopped her before she could finish. I didn't want to hear she'd made a mistake by telling me her feelings. I'd decided that it wasn't a bad thing to have things out in the open.

"Scarlett, how about you join Mia and I tonight for dinner?" I said, smiling down at Mia as she looked up at me and over to Scarlett.

"Oh, I couldn't."

I looked at her, my eyes falling to the items in her cart again.

"What do you think, Mia, should Scarlett come to dinner at our place tonight?"

Mia smiled and nodded, turning her attention back to her game.

"I think you should join us," I whispered again, this time winking at her. "I'm making my famous Thai crispy beef with vegetables."

Scarlett's eyes lit up. It had always been a favorite of hers, and so I'd always tried to make it when she was home from school.

"God, I haven't had that in years."

"So, I guess we can expect you around six?" I said,

glancing down at my watch, noticing that it only gave me a couple of hours to get things home and start preparing dinner. "Or will those peanut butter sandwich cookies and mango be sufficient?"

She looked around, then down to the things she'd apparently chosen for dinner and nodded. "Sounds good."

MIA AND SCARLETT headed into the living room while I cleaned up after dinner. I listened as Mia talked a mile a minute, showing Scarlett some of her favorite toys. I glanced in every few minutes to see Scarlett watching and listening with intent as Mia rambled on.

Mia hadn't been around many women, mainly because I never brought the odd date home. I didn't want to subject her to anyone who I didn't feel I could see myself having a long-term relationship with. Since I also didn't have many female friends, the only women Mia were around were Lorelai, Aurora, Peyton, Ella, Mrs. Fletcher and her grandmother. When I finished the dishes, I entered the living room, waiting until Mia finished showing Scarlett her collection of Disney movies.

"Alright, pumpkin, time for bed."

"But, Dad, I haven't shown Scarlett Potato."

I winked at Scarlett. "Do you think you can share Potato with Scarlett next time? It's already past your bedtime."

Mia let out a huff, placed her hands on her hips, and looked at Scarlett. "Dad always makes me go to bed early."

"Come on, let's go."

"Can you read me a story?" she said, coming over and taking me by the hand.

"A short one."

"Can Scarlett come?"

"I don't think Scarlett wants to hear a story."

"Sure, I do," Scarlett said, smiling at me and winking at Mia.

"Yay! Come on, Scarlett, you'll love Popcorn the Pug goes to the Movies. It's my most favorite story, Potato's too," she said, taking Scarlett by the hand and leading her down the hall and into her room.

I PULLED Mia's door partially closed, and both Scarlett and I headed back into the living room. Scarlett sat down while I pulled the blinds.

"Would you like a glass of wine?"

"Oh, I was actually going to get going," Scarlett said, looking down at her hands clasped in her lap.

There was no way she was leaving tonight without us talking about the other night.

"I think you should stay for some wine. I grabbed the bottle specifically for you," I said, leaving the room and heading to the kitchen to get us a drink and not giving her a chance to respond.

The moment I returned with the two glasses, she looked up at me, reaching for hers.

"Thank you," she said, her voice low.

"You're welcome. Shove over." I winked, watching as she shifted to the left for me to sit down.

She took a sip of her wine, then leaned forward, placing her glass on the table while I did the same, then I looked over at her. She could barely meet my eyes. I knew she was embarrassed about sharing her feelings, but she didn't need to be, not anymore.

"About the other night," I started.

"Levi, really, we don't have to talk about this. I should never have said anything. I don't know what it was I was doing," she said, getting up off the couch. "Really, I was in love with Duncan."

I grabbed her wrist, stopping her from getting up, and when she turned to look at me, I shook my head.

"Scarlett, you can say whatever you want, but I know you. I don't doubt you loved him, as a friend, but don't try to tell me now that you were in love with him because you've already told me the truth."

Scarlett slowly sank down to the couch, her eyes locked with mine.

"I spoke to Scottie," I admitted. "I'm sorry I couldn't crawl out of my head long enough to tell you how I felt about you."

Scarlett looked at me. I could see the questions in her eyes. I didn't want to rehash the past, anymore. We'd done that enough. I was ready to move forward. Without another word, I placed my hand on her cheek and took her mouth with mine, kissing her hard. When I finally pulled back, she was breathless, but the look in her eyes said it all. I stood up, taking her hand in mine and led her down the hall to my bedroom where I planned to take what I should have taken years ago.

Chapter 11

Scarlett

He shut the bedroom door, spun me around, and pushed me up against the bedroom wall. His eyes were full of want, lust, and need. He pressed his body against mine and claimed my mouth, his hand falling to my throat where his hand wrapped around my neck.

"I was a stupid man for waiting this long," he murmured, pressing his lips to mine while his fingers gently squeezed the side of my neck.

I could already feel the throbbing at my centre, my body begging for him to touch me in places I'd only ever dreamt he'd touch. He tugged at the button of my jeans as he lowered his hand from my neck, kissing his way down to the top of my shoulder as he slid his hand into my panties, running his finger through my slick centre. A moan escaped my lips as I closed my eyes and gripped his biceps.

"Open your eyes, Scarlett. I want you to look at me while I touch you."

When I opened my eyes, he pulled his hand from my pants and placed the two fingers he had buried inside of me into his mouth, licking them clean. My jaw dropped as he gave me that sexy grin I'd always loved.

"Get your ass over here," he said, sitting down on the edge of his bed.

With my legs shaking, I walked over and went to sit down, but he stopped me, placing his hands on my hips. He tugged my pants down over my hips, allowing them to pool at my feet.

"Take your shirt off," he commanded.

I did as I was told, lifting it up over my head, and when I looked back down at him, he too had removed his shirt. I could see the outline of his rigid cock through his jeans, something I'd felt so many times pressed into me while we'd been watching movies when we were younger.

He reached up, flicked the front clasp on my bra,

pushing it off my shoulders, then sat there, looking up at me.

He pulled me into him, pressing a kiss to each breast before laying back on the bed and undoing his pants, lifting himself just enough to shimmy his pants down.

I almost gasped when he sprung free. He was bigger and thicker than I'd expected. I bit my bottom lip as I watched him move to the centre of the bed, laying on his back, stroking himself.

Watching him, watching his head drop back, the taught muscles in his arm as he stroked himself, was probably the sexiest thing I'd ever seen. I couldn't keep my eyes off him.

"You going to come over here and join me?" he asked, still slowly stroking himself. "Perhaps sit on my face?"

"Levi…." I could feel my cheeks heating as I crawled onto the bed, and when I got closer, he placed his hand on mine.

"Crawl on top," he murmured. "I want to watch you."

I swallowed hard, "Levi, I—"

"Crawl on top of me. I want you on top for our first time. It will be easier for you if you take control. I've waited to long for this moment and if I take control, I won't be gentle, and I'll hurt you."

I swallowed hard as our eyes met. Then I crawled on top of him. He ran his fingers through my centre again, drawing small circles over my clit before sliding two fingers up inside of me.

"Fuck, Scarlett," he whispered, now taking his thumb and circling my clit while pumping his fingers inside of me.

I could already feel my orgasm building when he stopped. He reached over his head, grabbed a condom off his nightstand, opened it, and slid it over himself, then lined himself up at my entrance, running the tip of his cock through my centre.

"Go slow," he warned as I slid down on him, stopping as he stretched me to the point of hurting.

"God, Levi, it….it hurts," I moaned, biting my bottom lip as I allowed my body to adjust to the pain.

"Slowly," he reminded me, clasping my hands while I slowly pressed down on him a little more, stopping more often to give my body time to expand.

"Rub your clit," he whispered, looking in my eyes.

"I can't, Levi, it hurts."

"Rub your clit, Scarlett. It will take your mind off it and allow your body to relax."

While I wasn't a virgin, I certainly hadn't experienced this type of sexual relationship before. Duncan hadn't been vocal. He also hadn't been the type of man to tell you what he wanted or how to do something. I remembered most of my friends saying that he must be a boring lover.

"I want to watch you, Scarlett," Levi whispered.

I met his eyes, suddenly feeling very much on display as I thought about the position I was in. He didn't wait. He took my hand and placed my fingers between my legs where, with a nod from him, I gently touched myself.

I could feel my cheeks heat as I watched his eyes fall to my hand. My fingers danced over my clit.

"That's my girl. God, I love watching you touch yourself."

I bit my bottom lip as I watched him watching me and started lowering myself onto his cock, burying him deeper inside of me.

"Oh god, that's it, Scarlett." He moaned, gripping my hips, moving them back and forth as I rubbed my clit.

"Oh, fuck," I cried as I felt my orgasm building.

"That's it," he said breathlessly, slowing the movement of my hips.

He pulled my hand away, then sat up, wrapping his arms around me, and rolled us until I was laying against the mattress. He pulled his cock from inside me, letting me feel the emptiness.

He pushed my knees to my chest, then spread my legs open, first bending down and running his tongue through my centre. Flicking his tongue back and forth over my clit, before he slid two fingers deep inside of me.

"Ready for more?" he asked, looking up at me, taking his free hand and rolling my nipple between his fingers.

I moaned, this time stopping myself by biting the back of my hand, so we didn't wake Mia, and nodded.

Levi sat up, placed the head of his cock at my entrance, and started pushing forward. I figured I'd be able to take him faster, but he had to go slow again, allowing me to adjust to him. It didn't take as long, and once he was buried inside of me, he began thrusting his hips, bottoming out with each thrust.

"Rub your clit," he demanded again, breathless as he continued pumping deep inside of me. "I love to watch. I always want to watch."

I reached down and started circling my clit with my fingers, trying to hold my orgasm back from hitting. I bit my bottom lip, tipped my head back, and let out a loud moan as I felt myself tightening around him.

"Fuck, Scarlett, I'm going to come," he said, breathless as his muscles tightened and he poured into me, burying himself deeper than I thought was possible before collapsing on top of me.

One month Later

I TOOK a sip of my coffee after I'd just uploaded an article from the weekend and glanced down at my phone. I smiled when I saw Levi's name and opened our chat.

Levi: Not going to lie. It will be nice to be away this coming weeked and to have you there. Perhaps we can have a loud love making session the first night, you know, without little ears.

Scarlett: Is that so?

Levi: Yes, you know how it helps me to ease stress before and after a game.

I smiled. He wasn't wrong, he absolutely loved taking all his frustration out before and after a game, and I loved being on the receiving end.

Scarlett: Before, after, I'd even hedge a guess during if you could make that work.

Levi: Not during. I have to concentrate on the game, but I still think of you.

Scarlett: Good save ;) What time do you leave tonight?

Levi: I've got to beat the arena for six. You sure you'll be okay looking after Mia?

Scarlett: Of course. I'm looking forward to it.

Levi asked me if I'd be okay to watch Mia tonight while he played. Of course, I'd agreed immediately. I'd been spending a lot of time with Mia and Levi since the night I'd come for dinner. So much so, Levi had mentioned the guys were worrying because he'd not been out with them in a while. Tonight, he'd promised them he'd go out with them after the game.

Levi: Okay, because I'll be home late, remember I'm heading out with the guys.

Scarlett: I remember. It will be fine. I'll just crawl into your bed and wait for you once she is asleep.

Levi: Thanks for that visual, and on that note, I guess I'll let you get back to work. I have to get ready to go to a meeting. See you after work.

Scarlett: See you then.

I closed our chat and looked back to my computer to see an email had just come in. I opened my inbox to see Carol's name and froze as I read the subject line on the email. Apparently, Carol had contacted Skylar Payne on my behalf, and she had responded. Carol had forwarded me the email and as I sat there, I suddenly felt sick to my stomach. I took a deep breath and opened the email.

To Whom it May Concern,

I know you said this didn't require an in-person meeting, but I'll be in Vancouver in the next few days to take care of a legal matter. I could meet Scarlett Green on Wednesday morning, this week. I'd be happy to sit down and talk with her. I'm guessing the meeting is to talk about what transpired when I worked for the New York team and why I was fired. I follow the Ice Insiders and am aware of the pieces that have been going out on scandals in the sports community. I would be more than happy to tell my side of the story.

Sorry for the late response, Skylar Payne

I read her email over again. I had nothing to do with the articles she was speaking of, and Carol knew that, but I couldn't see the email Carol had sent to find out what it had said. As I read her email for a third time, I felt like I was going to be ill especially when I got to the part about a legal matter. I needed to get out of this, so I hit respond, and began typing, letting her know that I'd no longer need to meet with her when Carol stopped by my office.

"Scarlett, how are things coming with failure to commit article?"

I stopped typing, swallowed hard, and looked up at Carol who stood there grinning ear to ear. I wanted to confront her about this email but seriously doubted there was any point.

"Fine. Have one more interview to conduct and you'll have your piece."

"Perfect."

"I'll um, I'll need an extension."

Carol looked at me.

"The one interview I'm waiting on can't be held for two more weeks." I shrugged.

"Didn't you get my email?" she questioned.

"I did."

"Isn't that the interview you were waiting for?" she asked.

I looked at her and then at my computer screen. Honestly, I wasn't waiting for any interview, and I had a feeling she knew it. What I really wanted to tell her was to hold this damn interview herself since she was the one who'd contacted Skylar and by the looks of things under false pretenses. Instead of saying anything I just kept my mouth shut.

"Fine, a couple more weeks, but no more extensions after this one."

I nodded and watched her walk away, then turned back to the computer, tapping my nails on my desk.

I could only imagine how vague Carol had been in her email to her and how she had probably never mentioned Levi at all. It made total sense she was thinking it was about her being fired. Lately, the *Ice Insiders* had been doing many articles on things that had gone on in the past, and anyone who'd followed us and had been contacted for an interview would have the right mindset to think it was regarding a past event.

I shook my head and closed my email. I needed to think, and I needed air. I got up from my desk, called the front desk and told them to hold all my calls, then grabbed my jacket and took off from the office.

Chapter 12

Levi

Immediately upon entering Illusions, a staff member escorted us upstairs to our private room, where our food awaited us.

"Ah, food," Dylan said, heading over to the platter of hot wings.

"Fuck, I'm starved," I said, loading wings onto a plate as well.

Knox, Colton, Lucas, and Clay followed suit, and then we all took our usual seats. Colton took a minute to give everyone a beer.

I'd just sunk my teeth into one wing when Knox looked over at me.

"It's about time you join us," he said, drinking back half his beer.

"Yeah, sorry about that, guys. Things have been a little crazy." I shrugged.

"Who's the girl?" Colton questioned, taking a bite of pizza.

I looked at my teammates. They were waiting for me to divulge my secret. I could tell from the looks on their faces that they knew I was seeing someone, so there was no point in hiding it any longer. I was about to speak when Lucas cleared his throat.

"Don't even think about trying to tell us you aren't seeing anyone. We already know you are. Shitty game days, shitty practice days, not going out with us. Odd behavior there."

I sat back and let out a sigh. "Fine, yes, I am seeing someone."

"Who?" Colton questioned.

"I don't really think that matters, does it?" Dylan asked.

"Yep, it does. It will tell us on a scale of 1-10 how fucked up he really is," Knox answered. "I mean, look at Clay before I found out he was doing my sister."

"I was only fucked up because I knew you'd kill me," Clay said, shaking his head.

"Damn right I would. Should have kept it in your pants." Knox chuckled.

"Shouldn't you have kept yours in your pants, then? I mean, you were doing Phil's sister."

Knox looked over at Dylan and nodded. "Probably, but Lorelai had her shit together. Peyton didn't."

"Oh god, let it go already," Clay said, letting out an enormous sigh.

Knox laughed. "Just busting your balls."

"So, who's the chick?" Colton asked again, trying to get them focused on me.

I took a drink of my beer and sat back. "It's a little complicated, but it's someone from my past."

"An ex?" Colton asked.

I shook my head. "No, but it's a long story."

"Mia's mom?" Dylan questioned.

I shook my head. "No. If you want to know, it's an old friend's younger sister. I've known her since I was in my early teens, and we were practically inseparable growing up."

"Do we get a name?" Lucas asked, getting up and getting some pizza.

I knew the moment I told them her first name, they'd know exactly who it was, but I also knew they were relentless. They would get it out of me.

"Fine, but I don't want to hear any more after I tell you."

The guys all looked at one another in confusion and nodded.

"Her name is Scarlett."

The room was quiet. In fact, if it hadn't been for the rumble of music in the background, you'd probably have been able to hear a pin drop. They all looked at me, a load of questions I knew they were dying to ask.

"As in Green? The chick from the *Ice Insiders*?" Knox asked, not caring what he'd just promised.

I nodded my head.

"Fuck me," he said under his breath. "Don't you think it might be wise not to get involved with anyone in the media?" he questioned. "Or at least give us the heads-up when she started reporting on the team?"

"Whoa, now hold on," Dylan said. "We all know we can't help who we are attracted to."

"Never said we could. I'm just saying, this sort of thing could lead to a lot of trouble," Knox said as if I wasn't even in the room.

"Exactly, Knox, I'm with you on that. This could be disastrous for his career," Colton added.

"I wouldn't say disastrous," Lucas added. "But it might have a way of harming it."

"Whoa, guys, I'm right here, you know. I trust Scarlett. I've known her for a long time, and I know she respects my wishes, especially with the media. She knows how I feel about interviews and articles being written on me, and I know she would never break that trust."

"Yeah, until they bribe her or force her to write one on you."

"Wouldn't happen, trust me. I know this girl well. She'd come to me if they were trying to do something like that to her, besides I know she'd do nothing like that to hurt me or Mia."

"If you say so," Lucas said.

"Yeah, man, just be careful, okay?" Colton added.

I nodded. I knew this was coming from a place of caring, but right now, I didn't need those types of ideas in my head. Scarlett would never do something that would intentionally hurt me, that much I knew.

"I will be. Now, how about the game?" I said, changing the topic.

I OPENED MY EYES, blinking a few times as things came into focus. Scarlett rolled over and snuggled against me, her head on my shoulder. I pressed a kiss on her forehead and pulled her against me.

Things were progressing fast between us. I'd been

home most of the week, and she'd been here with us most of that time, aside from when she was working. I stroked her arm, and she let out a tiny moan just as Mia called for me.

"I'll be back," I whispered as I slipped from the bed. "Don't go anywhere."

I slid my shorts on and then left the bedroom, closing the door behind me, and went straight into Mia's room.

"What is it, pumpkin?" I asked.

"I had a bad dream," she cried, rubbing her eyes.

I walked over and picked her up, grabbing her blanket and Potato from her bed, carrying her into the living room where I flopped down in the corner of the couch, pulling her against me.

She rested her head on my chest and hugged Potato, while I covered her up with her favorite blanket before wrapping my arms around her.

"It's okay. It was just a dream. Close your eyes," I whispered, kissing her forehead.

Within minutes, Mia was back to sleeping soundly, and I carefully slid her off my chest down to the couch, got up, and went into the kitchen and started making some coffee.

I grabbed my pile of mail and carefully sorted through everything, one envelope, in particular, catching my eye. It was from a family law office in New

York addressed to me. Frowning, I ripped open the envelope and pulled out the letter inside just as I heard my bedroom door open. Not knowing what was on the letter, I quickly shoved it back into the envelope and shoved it into a drawer just as Scarlett came around the corner.

"Morning." She smiled.

"Morning. You ready for a full day?" I questioned.

We were getting together for lunch with Dylan and Aurora and Knox and Lorelai. They'd asked to meet Scarlett last night just before we left the club, and I'd reluctantly agreed, without even speaking with Scarlett until we got home.

Scarlett nodded and gave me a small smile.

"A little nervous. Is it okay if I go jump in the shower?"

"Of course. When you come back, I'll have your coffee ready." I winked, watching as she made her way down the hall.

The moment she was gone, I pulled out the letter and started reading it, a sick feeling forming in the pit of my stomach.

"UNCLE COLTY!" Mia yelled as Colton entered the backyard where we were all sitting.

Colton bent down and picked Mia up, throwing her up into the air as she laughed.

"Hey, Mia!" he said, tickling her once she was back safely in his arms.

Scarlett sat with Aurora and Lorelai, talking, each of them getting to know her and her them. Occasionally, she'd look over at me and give me a nervous smile. It wasn't a secret that the girls were on edge, but as always, they were doing their best to make Scarlett feel welcome, which I appreciated.

"Want another beer?" Dylan questioned, pulling me out of my own thoughts.

"Uh, yeah, I guess," I said, leaning forward to take the bottle from his hand.

"You guys are going to get it from Thompkins if you keep drinking this way during the season," Aurora called over.

She was right. We'd been hitting it a little hard, but right now, I didn't care. I needed to unwind today, especially after the letter I'd received this morning.

"Last weekend, promise," Knox called out, reaching into the cooler for another bottle just as Colton came over and grabbed one for himself.

"Glad you could make it," Dylan said, flipping the burgers on the barbeque.

"He isn't going to turn down free food." Knox chuckled.

"I see you aren't either," Colton responded, punching Knox in the bicep.

The guys laughed, but I just sat there, staring at the ground, lost deep in my own thoughts. I heard nothing around me, because all I could think about was that stupid letter stating that Skylar was coming for Mia. The sound of fingers snapping pulled me out of my head and I glanced up to see Dylan staring at me.

"What?"

"You going to answer Mia?" he asked, nodding over in her direction. "Before she has a full-on meltdown."

I looked over to see her holding something in her hands.

"What you got there?" I asked, getting up out of the chair I was sitting and making my way toward her.

She giggled as she opened her tiny hands to show me a little frog she'd caught.

"I found him. Can I keep him?" she asked, looking up at me with hopeful eyes.

"Oh, well, I don't think he'd be happy at home," I said.

"Yes, he can live in a jar. I will make him a bed and everything."

"No, sweet pea, he needs to be outside with all his

other frog friends. Now, how about we put him down in the flower bed over there?" I said, pointing toward Aurora's small garden while guiding her over to the corner.

She looked down at the small frog in her hand and sniffled.

"Sorry I can't take you home," she said to her hands, clasping them together as the frog tried to crawl away.

"Let him go right here." I pointed to a shady spot under one flower.

"Okay." She sniffled as she released the frog and watched him hop away.

I placed a kiss on her forehead, picked her up, and carried her over to the small sandbox Dylan had been working on for Jackson, then I made my way back over to the guys.

"So, you seem distraught. Everything okay?" Knox asked as I sat down.

I looked over at Scarlett to see she was knee deep in a conversation with Lorelai and Aurora and then looked back at the guys, who all sat there waiting for me to answer Knox's question.

"This doesn't leave this group."

"Got it," they all said in unison.

"I mean it, not a fucking word of it," I whispered.

The guys all looked at me, a seriousness falling over them.

"Got it," Dylan said, sitting down, leaning forward and resting his forearms on his knees.

"I got a letter this morning from a family law office in New York. Apparently, Mia's mom is coming after her."

The look on the guys' faces was the same as mine, and I could tell none of them knew what to say.

"When did you find this out?" Colton asked.

"This morning. The letter was in my pile of mail. Thing is, she's never been a part of Mia's life after she walked out that door, so I do not know how she even found me."

Colton glanced over his shoulder to where the girls sat, quickly drawing my attention to them.

"What about her?" he asked.

"No fucking way would she ever do something like that," I said with certainty in my voice.

"What are you going to do about it?" Dylan asked.

"Get myself a lawyer because there is no way she is taking Mia from me."

Chapter 13

Scarlett - Wednesday Morning

Levi hadn't been himself since early Sunday morning, and with each day that had passed, he'd become more withdrawn and tense. No matter how many times I'd asked him if everything was alright, he'd just nodded and told me not to worry, that it was just the stress of these upcoming games that had him on edge.

"You all packed?" I questioned, as I entered the kitchen to find him and Mia at the breakfast bar.

Levi nodded to the packed bags laying by the door. "Ready to go," he answered. "Mrs. Fletcher should be here shortly. No need to check in on them," he said, knowing I had a full week at work.

"I don't mind, Levi."

"No, you get your work done, and I'll see you in Boston on Saturday for the game, okay," he said, standing up and pouring me a cup of coffee into the travel mug for me to take.

"I want to go," Mia cried, looking up at us.

We both knew Mia had been having a hard time with Levi being gone lately. I only wanted to make it easier for her by popping in while he was gone, but he insisted it would only make things worse for her.

"You're staying with Mrs. Fletcher," Levi said, handing her a small bowl of raspberries from the fridge. "Say bye to Scarlett."

"Bye," Mia said, pouting as she waved, then went back to playing with her toys while she ate her fruit.

Levi walked me over to the door, wrapped his arms around me, and pressed his lips to mine. It was going to be four days before I could be in his arms again, which lately felt like forever when we were apart like this.

"Have a safe flight," I whispered, kissing him one more time before grabbing my bag at the door and heading off to the office, listening to Mia cry as I walked down the hall.

HAVING RESERVED the small boardroom for my interview with Skylar, I went in and quickly made two cups of coffee. I'd just finished when I received the notification that Skylar had arrived. Swallowing hard, hoping my stomach calmed down, I was about to leave the office and head to the front desk to get her when Carol came around the corner, a woman trailing behind her.

"Scarlett, I'd like you to meet Skylar Payne, I'll leave you two now." she said, immediately leaving the room, a sly smile on her face.

Of course, she was happy she was getting what she wanted; I thought to myself as I watched Skylar take a seat across from me.

"So, Skylar, I wanted to thank you for taking this meeting. However, it really wasn't necessary to come in person," I said, opening my notebook.

"It really wasn't a problem. It just happened to work out this way. I had some business to take care of here, anyway. So, you wanted to talk to me about what happened with the New York team."

Fuck, I'd forgotten that was why she thought she was called in here. I swallowed hard as I stared at my lined notebook.

"Sort of," I said, taking a sip of my coffee.

"Well, I'm not sure why you'd have called otherwise. It was for the sports scandal piece. At least, that was what I was told when I called your office, after you had reached out."

I sat there, surely looking like I was in shock. I'd not contacted Skylar, and now I was sat left wondering exactly what Carol had said in that email.

"Well, after I received your email asking for an interview, I called your office. The woman who I spoke with said it had to do with New York Enforcers." She smiled.

I looked down at the notepad in front of me as irritation seeped through me, then I looked over at Skylar.

She was a pretty girl and had a delicate figure, so it wasn't shocking to me that Levi would find her attractive, I thought to myself as I smiled back.

"Yep, you're right. It does," I said. "So why don't you tell me what happened?"

Skylar leaned back, wrapped her hands around her mug, and let out a sigh.

"Okay, well, let's see. I was a PR intern. I'd mistakenly got involved with the team's coach. We had been in a relationship about six months when I found out that he was married."

"Oh my, that must have been a shock to you," I said, making my notes.

"It was. His wife caught us in bed together one night while we were at an away game. Of course, when she walked in, I was mortified. She screamed at me, hit her husband, and while that all went on, I ran. I struggled with the fact that I'd probably lose my job when word got out, so I called in sick for a while, especially if I knew he was going to be around.

"Shortly after that, things finally calmed down, I was moved to work with one rep who dealt with the team members. It was easier for me to avoid the coach in this capacity. Once again, we were at an away game. I had to accompany Levi Anderson to a charity dinner. I'd followed his career even before I'd gotten hired and was beyond excited to get to spend time with him. I remember how charming he was at first, and if I'm honest, I might have even had a little crush on him. Although what girl doesn't have a crush on a hockey player?"

A hint of jealousy surged through me. I knew exactly what dinner she was talking about. I'd remembered seeing their pictures smeared all over, dancing together, laughing at this event. I was so jealous that I even remembered questioning him after seeing these pictures, wondering who she was. It was then Levi had told me about the one-night stand and told me not to get too upset. We weren't involved with one another yet and we were both allowed to date other people. One night as I stared at their photo together, I realized why it bothered me so much, and it was because while he was out dating others, I wasn't. I never told Levi that, but he knew how upset the news of him having a one-night stand made me and he promised me it would never happen again.

"He is charming, that is for sure." I winked, giving her a fake smile. "Go on," I urged.

"Well, that night, after we'd danced and had pictures taken, Levi had accompanied me back to the hotel and had walked me to my room. Once outside my door, something happened between us. Either I kissed him, or he kissed me, and the next thing I knew, we were in bed together. He snuck out before morning, and when I approached him at another event, two weeks later, he explained to me he was involved with someone and that the night we'd spent together would have to be our last.

"Weeks later, just when I thought things had passed, and I was involved with a wonderful player from Florida, word got around that I'd had relations with the coach, and others. Not only did my relationship come to an end but so did my employment before I even had a chance to explain."

"They didn't even ask you?"

"Okay, well, that isn't true. They asked me, but I couldn't lie about it, and the next thing I knew, my job was gone. Apparently, it was in my contract that there couldn't be fraternization."

"Wow, so what did you do?"

"Well, I couldn't work in those circles anymore. Those men basically ruined my career, but then the biggest shock of them all came. I found out a few months later I was pregnant. I knew it had to be Levi's after I'd visited my doctor, and I reached out to him. Only he wouldn't have anything to do with me. He said he was deep in a relationship and that I needed to go away."

I scribbled my notes as I tried to maintain a straight face.

"When I reached out to him again when I was just about at my due date, he refused to take my calls. So, then the baby was born, and I really struggled to look after her. I couldn't afford to raise her on my own, and I didn't have the money to go after him for support. Six months later, I ended up losing my apartment. With no job, I couldn't pay my rent, and Levi refused to speak to me. I at least knew where he lived, so one night I made my way across town and dropped the baby off to him. It was probably the hardest thing I'd ever done, giving her up, when all I really wanted was for him to help with her, but if I can be honest, I think he refused to believe it was his."

"Are you sure it was his?" I asked.

Skylar froze and glared at me as I looked up at her.

"I'm only asking," I said, certain I'd crossed a line I shouldn't have.

"Yes, I'm sure it's his."

"Okay."

"What are you doing now?"

"Well, I'm working in PR again, just not with a sports team. While this isn't a story that I'm proud of, women in the field need to know that this sort of thing happens in this industry, as I'm sure you know yourself."

"Right," I said. "Well, thank you for your time."

"You are welcome. When can I expect the article to air? I'd like to know that I've made people aware of what happened to me. I've spent years trying to get my name cleared."

"Well, legal will be in touch with you before it even gets printed, so watch for an email," I said, closing my notebook and getting up from where I was sitting and opening the door. The entire way to the front door, Skylar thanked me for talking with her and for wanting to bring her story to light.

I SAT behind my desk Monday afternoon, going over the article on Levi. I couldn't bash him how Carol had wanted, so I wrote nothing about anything I'd spoken to Skylar about. Instead, I focused on his career, highlighting his growth as a player with the Predators to his move to the Dominators. I wanted this article to be something he'd be proud of, not something he'd hate me for. Once I finished my final read-through, I attached a few pictures I'd had taken of him on the ice along with the article and submitted it to Carol, then gathered my things and made my way home.

Levi had just returned from his away games, and we were planning on taking Mia down to the waterfront festival. I quickly showered and then ran up to his unit. The moment he opened the door, he pulled me against him into an enormous hug.

"Fuck, I missed you," he whispered, meeting my lips with a tender kiss.

"I missed you too."

"Is Mia ready to go? It was getting busy down there."

"She's just over at the park with Mrs. Fletcher," he said, looking over his shoulder at the empty apartment, a mischievous grin coming to his face. "Which means we have the place to ourselves, at least for half an hour."

"Is that so?" I said, giving him a knowing look.

He placed his arm around me, closed the door, and we took off down the hallway to the bedroom.

I WATCHED Levi and Mia climb onto the teacup ride and took a seat, both waving in my direction. I smiled and waved back just as the ride started.

I looked out over the water, thinking about our afternoon quickie. I could still feel his hands gripping my hips as I sat on his face. I could still feel my orgasm rip through me as he relentlessly sucked my clit into his mouth while I gripped the headboard, screaming his name. He'd barely allowed me to come down from that orgasm before he was on his knees taking me from behind until we both collapsed on the bed, breathless.

"What are you thinking about?" I heard Levi say.

I turned my head to see him and Mia standing beside me.

"Not a thing," I said that, fully aware my cheeks were flushed. "How was the ride?" I asked Mia.

"It was AWESOME!!!! I want to do it again, but Dad says he is going to be sick," she said, covering her mouth as she giggled.

I looked at Levi, who shrugged his shoulders at me. "It's true, can't take the spinning."

"Please, Dad, just once more."

Levi looked at me again, then shrugged his shoulders.

"We'll be back." He sighed, getting back in line and handing over another few dollars to the attendant to allow them back on the ride.

"Have fun!" I yelled, laughing as they climbed onto the ride, this time choosing a different colored teacup.

This time as I watched them, I couldn't help but realize that Levi really was an amazing father. He gave Mia the world, and even though he wasn't always around, when he was, there wasn't a thing he wouldn't do for her. I watched as he did up the belt to secure her in and then tickled her tummy, causing her to break out in a fit of laughter while she tried to push his hands away. Then he wrapped his arm around her, pulled her close and kissed the top of her head.

Levi and I took turns taking Mia on all the rides, finally ending with a stop at the cotton candy stand where he got her and me a large bag of blue and pink colored sugary treat. We then walked hand-in-hand down the boardwalk while Mia walked in front of us.

"Thank you for today," he said, gripping my hand in his.

"You are welcome. I honestly couldn't have thought of a better way to spend an afternoon." I smiled.

"What was your favorite part?" he questioned, giving me that perfectly sexy grin of his.

I felt my cheeks heat at his question and could tell from the grin on his face that he already knew the answer.

"God, I love you," he said, then looked over at me with a shocked expression.

Immediately, I stopped walking, as did he, allowing the words he'd just spoken to sink into my mind.

I'd waited forever to hear him say those words to me, even though I knew it had always been something that had gone unsaid between us.

"I love you too," I replied, meeting his lips, sharing a tender kiss. Those words were the easiest words I'd ever spoken, rolling off my tongue like they were supposed to.

One week later

MIA SAT on the couch curled up between us as we watched *Finding Nemo*. We had spent the morning at the furniture store, looking for a new living room set that we both liked, then we stopped for breakfast where we began talking about moving in together again. Of course, we hadn't told Mia yet, but we were getting closer to finally settling on a date.

I had just put my phone down from reading an email when Mia told Levi and me to look at the TV because her favorite character was on the screen. Levi glanced up and then went right back to staring at his phone. He'd been catching up on his sports news since Mia had wanted to watch the movie instead of the Sports Channel.

I glanced over at him to see him shift uncomfortably in his seat, the color in his face draining. I knew something was wrong when his hand dropped away from the back of my neck where he'd kept it the entire evening while we'd been watching TV together.

"What is it?" I questioned, watching him with concern.

He looked over at me. Something was wrong, I could tell from the look in his eyes.

"Levi? What is it?" I asked.

I swore his eyes got darker as he looked at me, and then he glanced down at Mia, only to look back at me.

"We'll discuss it later," he gritted, looking back to his phone just as someone knocked on his door. Without another word, Levi left his phone on the couch, got up, and made his way to the kitchen.

My curiosity grew as I reached over and grabbed

his phone, looking down at the article he'd been reading. There, in black and white, was the article header Carol had wanted me to use; Levi Anderson: Reliably Unreliable, written by Scarlett Green.

Panic filled me as I read through the article. It wasn't the article I'd submitted. As I continued reading, my mind raced as I realized every word I'd submitted was gone. Carol had rewritten the entire article, or she had someone else do it for her just as she'd threatened, only she attached my name to the article.

My stomach turned as I stared at his phone, the words blurring. There was information and snippets from my notes from my conversation with Skylar in there. She must have gone into my computer and read the notes I'd made.

"Can we watch it again?" Mia shouted.

I looked up to see the credits rolling on the TV.

"Not right now, maybe in a bit," I said, moving Mia off my lap. I got up, flipping the TV to the cartoon channel for her.

"Mia, you stay here and watch some cartoons, okay? I'm gonna go find your dad," I said, putting on one of her favorite shows and leaving her on the couch with Potato.

"Okay, don't be gone too long," she sang and then giggled, throwing Potato up in the air.

Mia talked to herself as I made my way into the kitchen to see the door to the condo ajar. I could hear Levi talking. His voice wasn't loud, more like a mumble, but I could tell whoever was at the door had aggravated him.

I pulled the door open, and that was when Levi whipped around and glared at me. His shoulders were tense, his back straight, even the muscles in his forearms were taught from the pile of paperwork he held in his hands. Whatever was going on out here wasn't good. The tension was so high you could feel it in the air.

"Go inside, I'll be right in," Levi grumbled.

I was about to turn and go back inside when I heard a woman's voice. "It's you."

I poked my head back around the doorframe to see Skylar standing there, her arms crossed in front of her, a manilla envelope in her hands.

So, this was the legal issue she had to take care of. Was she here to get custody of Mia? Surely, she couldn't take her away from Levi, could she? I tried to pretend I didn't know what she was talking about, but then Levi grabbed my arm and looked at me.

"You know one another?" he questioned.

"No," I quickly said and went to head back inside, trying to get away from what I already knew was coming.

"Yes, we know one another. She just did an interview with me about what happened with my job at the New York Enforcers. She works for the *Ice insiders*."

I could feel my stomach turn. This was all wrong, and I wanted to shout at Levi and tell him everything. We hadn't even talked about the article he'd just seen, now this.

"So, let me guess, you're the reason Skylar is in town?" he growled, the look on his face one I'd never wanted to see.

"No."

"You're the reason she's here trying to get custody of a child she's barely laid eyes on. What did you promise her if she did the interview?"

"Levi, believe me, I didn't—"

"Just go inside!" he yelled.

I could feel Skylar's eyes on me, I wanted nothing more than to crawl into a hole and die. I stepped back into the apartment and closed the door, making my way down the hall to the bedroom, where I sat down on the edge of his bed and looked at the floor, praying he'd give me a chance to explain.

"Scarlett…" I heard Mia's voice say as I got up and folded my clothes, placing them in my overnight bag.

It was probably best if I gave Levi some space, at least for a couple of days, I thought to myself.

"Yes, Mia?"

"Where are you going? I thought we were going to the park today?" she asked, coming into the bedroom and crawling up onto the bed with Potato in her arms.

"Not today, sweetheart."

"But you promised."

Yes, she was right, I'd promised, but that was before my world blew up.

"I know, sweetie, but something has come up and I need to go." I sniffled.

"Daddy says when you promise someone something you should follow through."

I looked down at her face, brushing her hair behind her ears.

"Why are you so sad, Scarlett?" she asked.

"Mia, go to your room," Levi barked, causing both of us to jump.

"But, Daddy, Scarlett promised to take me to the park and now she is sad."

"Mia, to your room now!" Levi yelled, raising his voice.

Mia looked up at me, tears now streaming down her face, and slid off the bed, crying as she ran past Levi and slamming the door to her room. I could hear her cries in the distance as I looked at Levi.

"Levi, please, let me explain," I cried.

"Reliably Unreliable, that's what you think of me?"

"Levi, I swear to you I never submitted that article," I cried, moving toward him, wanting to hug him and apologize for what Carol had done.

"Don't come near me." he said, backing away. "I should have fucking known better than to get involved with you again. I found it odd you were out here to begin with, and that was why I guarded myself and acted like an ass. Apparently, I had been wise to do so."

"No, you weren't. I didn't do this, believe me," I cried, my throat getting tighter as I stood there. "I wrote about your career, highlighting all the amazing moments."

Levi ran his hands through his hair, turning away from me for a moment, before he turned back to face me.

"I allowed you into my life, into Mia's life. I let you into our world, to have you do this? You're going to find out just how reliably unreliable I am. Now, because of you and the shit you've caused, the interview you ran, I have to fight Skylar for custody of Mia."

"Levi, please, let me explain. Let me prove to you I didn't do this."

Levi was quiet as he glared at me while Mia cried in the distance. I hated hearing her cry, and I hated the way I felt right now. She was crying because of me. My chest hurt, my head felt fuzzy, and I felt sick to my stomach thinking about how much hurt I'd caused the pair of them.

"I don't want to hear your bullshit. I think it's better for everyone if you just take your shit and get the hell out."

Tears flooded my eyes as I stood there looking at Levi. "You don't really mean that, do you?" I sniffled.

Levi turned away from me, not saying anything.

"Levi?"

"I'm taking Mia to the park. We'll be gone for an hour. When we get back here, I don't want to see anything that reminds me of you in this apartment. Don't call me, don't text me, don't talk to me at games, and if you don't have that article retracted, not only will the *Ice Insiders* be hearing from my lawyer, but you will be as well."

Immediately, he made his way to Mia's bedroom and went inside. He was in there for a few minutes before I heard her sobs stop, and then they appeared in the hallway, Mia looking over Levi's shoulder at me. She lifted her little hand and waved, wiping at her tear-filled eyes as he carried her away from me.

Then they were gone.

Chapter 14

Levi

After I'd put Mia down for the night I got on the phone with my lawyer, not only about the article, but about custody. He immediately started working on things, and now all I needed to do was to calm down and let him take care of things.

I'd just sat down on the couch with a cold beer when someone knocked on the door.

"That had better not be Scarlett." I mumbled to the empty room, getting up, making my way to the door.

I pulled it open to see Dylan, Knox, Colton, Lucas,

and Clay all standing in the hallway. Clay held a case of beer, Dylan held two boxes of pizza, and someone must have a box of wings because I could smell the sauce from The Rusty Anchor.

"What the hell are you guys doing here?" I asked, knowing that tonight was one of our two nights off before we were hitting the road for four days.

"Well, we saw the article, figured it might be best if we come on by as opposed to texting."

"Yeah, because the support we give one another through text is truly lacking." Clay chuckled.

"That's your opinion Clay. I think our chat support is stellar." Knox added.

"Come on in, but we'll have to keep it down. Mia's asleep," I said, glancing back at her bedroom door as the guys all piled into the kitchen.

I went and pulled her door closed and then returned to the kitchen where the guys were already piling food onto plates before we made our way into the living room.

"How are you doing?" Dylan asked once we were all sitting down.

"Trying to keep it together. I've already contacted Harvey and he's working on things as we speak."

"Think Skylar will get custody?" Colton questioned.

I shook my head. "Harvey says she doesn't have a

chance. Even if we have to pay her to go away, he says the courts will never grant her custody with her lifestyle the way it is."

"That must ease your mind," Clay added.

"It does." I nodded.

"What about the article?" Knox questioned. "I couldn't believe what I read. Lorelai was appalled. She immediately turned to me and said how she felt that she couldn't trust Scarlett."

"Harvey is sending out an immediate retraction notice, otherwise he's starting a lawsuit for defamation, and not only will we be going after the *Ice Insiders* but after Scarlett as well."

"Thank god for Harvey," Dylan said, raising his beer in the air in a mock cheer.

The room grew quiet as the guys all looked at me, the unasked question hanging in the air.

"We're over, because I know you guys are wanting to know."

The guys all nodded. Each one of us knew what it was like to lose someone, and even though she'd done what she'd done, and I was angry, I was still hurt and upset that something that had been wonderful at one point was now over.

"Sorry, man," Clay said.

"Yeah, we're sorry," Colton said.

"Thanks, but really, I should have known better.

Things never progressed between us for a reason. I guess it's true what they say about the past and how you should never revisit it."

Dylan got up and patted me on the shoulder. "Want some food now?" he questioned.

I'd not eaten since breakfast, and for the first time all day, my stomach let out a grumble. "Yeah, I think I'll join you guys."

"I'll get you a plate. I'm going that way anyway."

I looked around at all my teammates, my friends, and suddenly felt very blessed to have such wonderful family.

"Now, before we move off to another topic, we need to know, is it true that you are looking at moving to another team?" Colton questioned.

God, it only got worse, I thought to myself as I remembered reading that part in the article. "Fuck no, I just moved here. I like the team, the city, and most of all I love all you asses. I am not nor do I have plans of moving until the team wants to kick me to the curb."

"Thank you! I told you idiots that had to be false information." Colton chuckled, looking at all the other guys.

Dylan came in and passed me my plate, and I dove into the food with a vengeance, realizing just how hungry I was.

Chapter 15

Scarlett

My world had come to a crashing halt. I had no idea what to do. I'd spent most of the week in bed, called in sick to work, and had barely gotten up to eat. I was gutted and literally felt as if I were going to die.

I opened my eyes, glanced around my messy bedroom, looking at all the dirty clothes that lay in piles on the floor. My stomach hurt from not eating, but at the same time, the thought of food made me sick. I rolled over, facing the window, catching my reflection. I was a disaster, and I really needed to get up and take a shower.

Digging deep within myself, I slipped from my bed and headed into my ensuite, starting the shower. I shed my robe and climbed in, welcoming the warmth of the water over my aching body.

I took my time drying and styling my hair and putting on makeup, then got dressed. I made my way out into my apartment, grabbed my keys, and made my way into the office.

The receptionist greeted me as I walked in, but I said nothing. I'd come here to do one thing and one thing only: confront Carol. I marched down the hall toward her office and barged through her closed door.

She lifted her head from her computer at the intrusion, a look of irritation on her face.

"Scarlett! Don't you know how to knock?"

"Cut the crap. Of course, I know how to knock," I barked.

I slammed her office door shut behind me, making my way to the edge of her desk.

"Don't you dare take that tone with me!" she yelled.

Someone needed to take a tone with her after what she'd just done to me. I hovered over her. I was done with her attitude and being held under her thumb.

"How dare you!" I yelled.

"How dare I what?"

"The article!" I screamed, anger coursing through me.

"Oh, that." She laughed. "Scarlett, don't get your panties in a twist."

I frowned as I looked down at her. My panties in a twist? Did she just say those words as she laughed at me? Why would she find any of this funny?

"Scarlett, I simply polished the article you turned in."

"Polished it? You changed every single word of it."

Carol sat there, looking up at me, her hands under her chin.

"What I did was write a better article, one that has gotten more attention than you'd have ever gotten with the piece you wrote. You are welcome," she said, picking up her pencil, making some notes in her notebook.

"I can't believe you would actually do that!"

Carol shook her head. "Why can't you believe it? I wasn't printing the garbage you gave. I told you I wanted real and raw. I wanted the truth. You failed."

Anger flooded me. "I didn't fail, I just didn't give you what you wanted."

"Precisely. You didn't turn in what I asked for, therefore, you failed. Just like I knew you would."

"What is that supposed to mean? Like you knew I would?" I asked, shocked she'd say something like that.

"Scarlett, I wanted to test you, because I didn't think you'd have the balls to write what I wanted. I was right."

"There was nothing wrong with the piece I wrote."

"Scarlett, there were so many things wrong with it. It was lacking, it was weak. It's almost as if he were an old family friend or something and you didn't dare want to cross a line."

I bit my lip as anger flooded my body. She had no right to do what she'd done. She certainly had no right to put my name on the article she'd written.

"Oh, and as for the position with the *Ice Insiders*, we've given it to Luke."

I could feel the tears burning in my eyes as I looked at her. "Well, congratulations to Luke," I said, swallowing every emotion I was feeling.

My mind spun as I stood there looking at that smug smile that sat on her face. A smile I wanted to smack right into next week.

"Now, about your next assignment…"

Carol continued talking but I heard nothing as I stood there, trying to get a grasp on myself and how I felt.

"Well, what are your thoughts?" She questioned me, pulling me out of my thoughts.

"Honestly, I really don't think this is the place for me anymore."

"What do you mean?" Carol asked, looking at me as if I'd just announced something she hadn't been expecting.

"Consider this my last week."

"You're giving me one week's notice?" Carol asked, straightening up in her seat.

"No, today is my last day. I'm done."

Carol looked at me and chuckled. "Ah, so quit when things get tough. Exactly what I thought. You really don't have the guts to be a reporter with us."

"I guess I don't," I said, turning and walking over to her door, ripping it open. "Actually, Carol, I have the guts, but what I don't have the guts for is working for a person or company who is okay with potentially harming people's careers and personal lives intentionally for their own personal gain."

"We'd never," Carol said, looking shocked at my accusation.

"Funny, because you did just that. Now I am going to clean out my desk."

I COULD FEEL the box I was carrying slip out of my arm as I struggled to get my keys from my purse. I lifted a knee to stop the box from falling as my keys got stuck in the handle of my bag.

"Fuck," I muttered under my breath.

"Here, let me help," I heard someone say and turned to see Mrs. Fletcher coming over to me.

She took the box from my hands while I untangled my keys from my bag and slid the key into the lock.

"Thanks," I mumbled, taking the box from her as I stepped into the apartment.

"Will you be coming up to see Mia tonight?" she questioned, poking her head into my unit.

Levi was supposed to travel this weekend, and it had become a common practice that I'd pop up and Mrs. Fletcher and I would take Mia over to the park for a couple of hours.

"No, I'm afraid not. Levi and I are no longer together," I answered.

"Oh dear, that would explain his mood as of late. I'm sorry to hear that. You two made a good couple. I was hoping we'd have heard wedding bells soon."

I nodded. That was what I'd thought to, but the universe had other plans.

"Thanks. I take it you're staying with Mia tonight while Levi travels."

"Yes, are you going to the game?"

I shook my head. "No, I'm afraid not. I quit my job today, hence the box of things."

Mrs. Fletcher stepped inside and looked at me. "Dear, is everything alright?"

"I'm moving back home with my parents for a while until I can get back on my feet. Once I'm away from here, away from Levi, everything will be okay."

"Oh, well, I'll be sad to see you go." She said, opening her arms for a hug.

I stepped into her arms and hugged her back. "Thanks, I'll miss you as well. I don't want you to be late." I said, glancing at the clock.

"Oh dear, you're right."

She hugged me goodbye, and then I shut and locked the door behind her and looked around. I loved this apartment, and I really loved this city, but I couldn't stay here. I couldn't pick up my life and move on, especially if I was living in the same building as the man who owned my heart.

Chapter 16

Levi - One Month Later

I'd dropped Mia off at daycare and walked into the change room, immediately heading to my locker to get ready for afternoon practice.

"Bout time you got here," Knox said, bumping me with his shoulder.

"I know. Mia had a mini meltdown just before we left."

"My little bean alright?" Colton asked, shoving his things into his locker.

"Yeah, just another missing Scarlett moment. I'll be so happy when she forgets about her." I sighed, sitting down on the bench to take a breath.

"She still going on about that?"

I nodded. "She even cried herself to sleep the other night," I said, running my fingers through my mop of curls.

"Maybe a night at Uncle Knox and Aunt Lorelai's would help?" Knox said, sitting down and lacing his skates. "Lorelai would love to have her. She was talking about taking her for a mani-pedi the other day to that new spa that opened."

Lorelai had stepped up recently, offering to take Mia and do things that Scarlett had done with her, just to keep some sort of balance in her life. I was beyond grateful.

"Careful, I may take you up on the overnight offer." I chuckled, pulling off my shirt.

"Practice in five!" Coach Thompkins yelled from the door.

I looked down at myself. I wasn't even close to being ready, thanks to Mia's minor meltdown. "Fuck, you guys go. I'll be there in a few minutes," I said, not wanting the rest of them to be late because of me.

The second the guys left the locker room, and I started changing, my phone rang. I looked at the screen and saw Harvey's name. The *Ice Insiders* had retracted the article almost faster than when they printed it, but this one was the call that I'd been waiting for.

"Hey, Harvey," I greeted.

"Levi, so glad I caught you. Listen, things are just

about finished with the custody agreement, but I wanted to talk to you before I signed on your behalf."

"Okay."

My stomach flipped. I'd been on edge for the past six weeks waiting to hear from him. Of course, he'd kept me updated via email, but I'd yet to speak with him.

"Listen, Skylar will drop this entire thing, but she wants payment in return."

I shook my head and pinched the bridge of my nose. She wanted payment. So typical, I thought to myself.

"What does she want?" I asked, afraid to know the answer.

"In the grand scheme of things, it's not a lot of money."

"What's not a lot of money, Harvey?" I questioned, mentally preparing myself for the figure.

"She'll go away and never come near you again for one point five million."

I leaned back against the lockers and shook my head. Her belief that she deserved money after I raised Mia astonished me.

"Levi, if I can offer anything, I think you should do it. Get her off your back and out of your life and move on," Harvey said.

"Fine, but she needs to sign an agreement stating

she can't turn around and come after me again," I bit out.

"Already in my hand, Levi. No worries there. Consider it done."

"Thanks, Harvey. Oh, and if you can get her to agree for a million, I'd appreciate it."

"Do my best, Levi. Talk soon."

I HONESTLY FELT like my life was finally turning back to normal. Weeks passed, Mia finally stopped asking about Scarlett, and Skylar had taken the one million and signed the paperwork. I'd never been so relieved. The one thing I feared the most was losing Mia.

I'd just finished a slew of away games, and we were now on mid-season break, which meant I had nowhere to be for at least a week.

I slipped from bed and got into the shower. It was still early, but I wanted to get a head start on vacation. I was taking Mia home to see my parents for a few days before life returned to normal.

Once I showered, I made my way to the kitchen to make special animal waffles for breakfast. It was a tradition that I'd started, we had animal waffles the first day of mid-season break. Then we were heading to the airport for our flight to New York.

I had just poured the batter into the waffle iron when my phone pinged. I figured it was the guys, I grabbed it and opened my app to see Scottie's name.

Scottie: Can we talk?

I tapped the edge of my phone and then opened the waffle iron, removing the first waffle. I added more batter and shut it before responding.

Levi: If it's quick, yes. Busy day ahead.

Immediately, my phone rang, and I grabbed it, hopefully before it woke Mia. She was still asleep, and I always enjoyed seeing the look of surprise on her face when I placed the plate of animal waffles in front of her.

"What's up?" I questioned.

"Levi, we need to talk."

"About?"

"Scarlett…"

I closed my eyes. The last thing I wanted to do was to have a conversation with Scottie about his sister's actions. I was still pissed with everything that had gone down, and I knew I would have a hard time not telling him exactly how I felt.

"Levi, she's crushed."

"She should be," I bit out.

The last thing I wanted to hear was how hurt she was because of something she did herself, because, frankly, she wasn't the victim here.

"Did you give her a chance to explain?"

"No. Why the hell would I?"

"Levi, she didn't do the things you think she did. It was someone else."

I was seriously beginning to think she was a master at getting people to believe her lies. I questioned everything we ever had between us. I certainly had to second-guess her sob story about her and Duncan and the fact that she never loved him. For all I knew, that was nothing but a crock of shit to weasel her way into my life. Now that I thought about it, I was even more disappointed with myself that it had worked.

"Is that what she told you? A sob story to get you to believe her, so she doesn't come out looking like the bad guy, but a victim in all this as well?"

"Levi, come on, man."

"Scottie, to be honest, I don't want to hear it."

The line was quiet for a moment, and then Scottie cleared his throat.

"Levi, listen. She quit her job and moved home."

"Convenient, add on more pity Scarlett vibes. And I should care, why?"

"You should care because those aren't actions of someone who would do something like that on purpose. She wants to call you, to explain some things to you, but she's afraid you won't talk to her."

"At least she's smart in that regard, because she's right. I won't talk to her. It's her actions that caused me to have my name dragged through the mud, to almost lose some contracts because of her, and it also caused me to almost lose Mia. If she's smart, she'll stay the hell away from me."

"All she wants is a chance to apologize, Levi. Give her that."

I couldn't help but chuckle. Did he honestly think I was that stupid, that I'd want to sit down and listen to more lies that fell from her lips?

"Scottie, I hate to do this because I've always considered you to be one of my best friends. However, your sister has just cost me a tremendous amount of hurt and a fuck of a lot of money, and I'm serious when I say she needs to stay away. I'm also going to tell you that if the only time you are going to call me is when you feel the need to advocate for her, don't fucking bother."

The phone was silent as I waited for him to respond. Those words probably hurt me more than ever, since we'd been friends for as long as we had, but the part of my life that contained Scarlett was over and I was ready to move on. I was just about to say something when I heard Mia's small voice behind me.

"Morning, Daddy!"

I didn't stay on the phone. Instead, I hung up and made my way over to Mia.

"Morning, Pumpkin," I said, quickly kissing her on the head, then opening the waffle maker before the waffle burned. I went around the island and picked her up, hugging her tight, then placing her on her chair. "How about some animal waffles?" I said, placing the plate in front of her with two waffles outlined like cats.

She covered her mouth and giggled as she pulled Potato close to her. "Look, Potato, kitty waffles." She giggled.

I couldn't help but smile as I went back around and poured more batter into the waffle iron, then poured us both a glass of juice.

"READY TO WATCH THE VANCOUVER GRIZZLIES?" I asked Mia as we followed my parents down the steps of the stadium to our seats.

Mia nodded her head. I'd gotten her one of the baseball jerseys as a surprise before we'd left Vancouver, knowing we'd be hitting the season opener while we were visiting my parents in New York.

The moment we were in our seats and Mom and Dad sat down, I handed Mia to Mom.

"Who wants drinks and food?" I questioned.

"I'm dying for a ballpark dog, as is your mother," Dad said.

"Me too!" Mia shouted with excitement.

"You too?" I said, tapping her small baseball hat as I made a face at her, causing her to laugh.

"Dad, you're silly."

"Alright, I'll be back. Mia, stay with Grandma and Grandpa," I said, leaving to make my way back up the stairs and to the line for the concession stand.

Once in line, I quickly checked my messages, responding to the boys about our return flight, and then pocketed my phone just in time to hear a woman's voice call my name. Reluctantly, I turned around to see Scarlett standing behind me. I said nothing as I stared at her.

"It's good to see you," she said, as if nothing had happened between us at all.

"Someone's opinion may differ from that," I bit back, turning around and placing my order with the vendor.

"What are you doing out here?" she questioned.

"Visiting my parents. Want to write an article about that now?"

"Levi, please, I've been wanting to apologize to you. I left my job at the *Ice Insiders*."

"Great, I'm happy for you. Hope they are treating you like the trash you are where you're working."

Scarlett looked at me. I could see the tears forming in her eyes. Perhaps I was being beyond harsh, but fuck, she's ripped out my heart and went straight for the jugular by betraying my trust.

"Look, Scarlett, I'm not gonna sugar coat shit. You tore my heart out, and not only mine, but Mia's. I can forgive myself for being stupid enough to let you back into my life, but I can't forgive myself for allowing Mia to fall in love with you. The tears she has shed over you broke me even more because I know it was my fault for allowing you into her life. So, as sorry as you are, and regardless of what truly happened, you need to understand that there is no way I can do this right now. The hurt's been caused, and the damage done."

"Levi…" she whispered, placing her hand on my forearm, which I pulled away.

"Sir, your order is ready," the guy behind the counter said, tapping my shoulder.

I turned, thanked him, and took the box of food from him, and went to walk away when I felt a tap on my shoulder. Scarlett stood there looking up at me, tears in her eyes, one even escaping and rolling down her cheek.

"I hope you can find it in your heart to forgive me one day, Levi."

I shook my head as I looked at her. "Have a good life," I said and made my way over to the staircase that led to our seats, joining my parents and Mia, forgetting about the confrontation I'd just had.

Chapter 17

Scarlett

"You look deep in thought. What are you working on?" Scottie asked, coming into the kitchen and heading for the fridge.

"I didn't think you were still here," I said, turning and looking at him over my shoulder.

"Mom tricked me into staying, bribing me with her pineapple upside-down cake."

I nodded. "Ah, yes, I had to leave the table. She's making me gain weight. I told her she needs to stop making all the sweet treats." I giggled.

It had been six months since I'd returned home.

While my life hadn't come back together after all that had happened, I was slowly healing. I still held onto the feelings I'd had the day I left Vancouver. Levi wasn't a person you got over quickly. In fact, I missed him, and Mia so much and still thought about them every day. Scottie once told me it takes thirty days to get over someone, but he'd been wrong. No matter how many text messages I'd typed out containing an apology or explanation, I sent none of them. I knew Levi would never respond to them anyway, so I figured why face even more hurt?

Scottie pulled the chair out from beside me and sat down, cracking open a can of cola. "So, what are you working on?" he asked, looking at my screen to see a video of the Dominator's last game. Of course, I'd conveniently paused the game right when Levi was on the screen.

"Nothing, just catching up on the games." I shrugged, looking over at my brother, forcing a smile.

"Have you spoken to him?" Scottie questioned.

I shook my head. "No, only at the ball game a few months ago. To be honest, even if I did, I wouldn't even know what to say to him. So, it's pointless. He's so angry at me."

"Well, what are you going to do about it?"

I shrugged my shoulders. "I doubt there is anything I could do."

"Well, maybe you should come up with some ideas. Make it a work in progress?"

I looked at my brother, let out a sigh, then lifted my notebook, pulling out a piece of paper with some ideas I'd written with ways to apologize to him.

"What's this?" he asked.

"This is what I've come up with," I said, shoving my list to Scottie.

He looked at it, then chuckled as he looked over at me.

"What's so funny?"

Scottie shifted in his chair and picked up the piece of paper and began reading out loud.

"Number 1. Move to a new state. You did that, it hasn't helped." He winked. "Number 2. Go on an Eat, Pray, Love type journey to find myself. I can't for the life of me see you going to any of those places she visited in that movie, aside from maybe Italy. Number 3. Go on a yoga retreat. I love you, Scar, but how are any of these going to help you apologize to Levi?"

I shrugged my shoulders. "I don't know. Maybe if I find myself, I'll have the courage to text him and apologize."

Scottie shook his head. "Okay, Number 4. Be hypnotized to forget all past life experiences that relate to Levi." He looked over at me and placed the paper on the table, shaking his head.

"What?" I questioned.

"While all these things are great ways to heal yourself after what's happened, aside from the hypnotic experience, if you really want to apologize, it needs to be something big, and it needs to come from here," he said, placing his hand over his heart.

I looked down at the list on the table. He was right. This list was garbage. I reached over and crinkled up the paper and looked at my brother.

"I don't have a clue what to do. He was so horrible when I saw him last."

"He's hurt, Scarlett. What I think you need to do is take some time to think about it. Let your heart lead you. Do what comes naturally."

"What if it doesn't work?"

Scottie got up and slid the chair back under the table. Placing a hand on my shoulder, he leaned down and kissed the top of my head.

"If it doesn't work, then you two weren't meant to be, and you'll need to find a way to move on. At least you can make peace with yourself knowing you tried."

"Thanks," I whispered, looking back at the screen.

"Scarlett, from here," Scottie said, tapping his chest once again before he left me in the kitchen.

I TOOK to heart what my brother had suggested, finally sitting down and writing everything out, from my heart. When I finally finished everything, I attached the document to an email and sent it over to my brother to get his opinion before I moved forward.

I sat behind my desk, the office buzzing with energy, when my phone rang.

"Scarlett Green, how can I help you?" I answered.

"Scar, that was amazing!" Scottie boomed.

"You like it?"

"You hit it out of the park."

"Well, if it hadn't of been for you, I'd probably be stuck in some place on the other side of the world hating myself." I giggled. "You really think it's good?"

"I do. Now, when are you sending it to him?" he questioned.

I sat there, unsure how to answer, biting my thumb. I'd come up with an idea but I wasn't sure it was the right way to go about this.

"Scar, you there?"

"I'm here."

"When are you sending it?"

I closed my eyes and took a deep breath. "I'm not."

The line went quiet. I'm sure my brother probably thought I'd gone crazy. I'd spent all this time on this, and now I wasn't going to send it.

"You mean to tell me you've gone to all this trouble agonizing for months over him and you're just going to shove this into the bottom drawer?"

"Have you spoken to him?" I questioned.

"Scarlett, what are you thinking?" Scottie asked.

"Just answer me."

"I have. Just the other day, in fact. Why?"

I looked at the calendar on the wall, at the date I'd circled two weeks ago. It had been my way of giving myself a deadline.

"Do you know if he's seeing anyone?" I asked.

"Scarlett?" my brother repeated. I could hear the tension in his voice. "What are you going to do?"

"Just answer me."

"No, he isn't seeing anyone," Scottie said, letting out a huff. "Now, what are you going to do?"

I tapped the tip of my pen on the circled date and pinched the bridge of my nose as I leaned back in my chair. If this blew up in my face, I'd have to leave the publishing world.

"I'm going to have them print the article, and then I'm heading to Vancouver to cover the playoff game between Floridaand them."

The line went quiet. I knew the risk I was taking by

doing this. I certainly didn't need to hear anything from Scottie.

It was then the editor of the journal I wrote for poked her head into my office, giving me a thumbs-up regarding the article I'd just submitted. I covered the receiver and pulled the phone away from my ear.

"All good?" I questioned.

"It was great, best thing I've read in a while. It will go out when you requested." She winked.

"Thank you."

She nodded, pulling my door closed, and I brought the phone back to my ear.

"You there?" I questioned, the line still quiet.

"Just be careful, Scarlett. I don't know how Levi will react to this."

I didn't know how he'd react either. That was what I was worried about the most.

"Noted. I've got to run. I'll call you soon."

I hung up the phone, looked over at the date circled on the calendar. Only ten more days. I also had accepted the fact that this would be my last attempt at an apology, and if it didn't work, I'd have to allow myself to let go of the dream of us being together, and move on with my life.

Chapter 18

Levi

"What a crazy week!" I said to Dylan and Aurora as we made our way into the arena.

They had picked me up from the airport an hour ago. Mrs. Fletcher had gotten news that her daughter who lived in Halifax was having some health issues, so I'd had no choice but to take Mia to New York to stay with my parents. I'd flown there yesterday, spent the night, and flew back today in time for our first playoff game against Florida.

"Well, it's going to be another crazy couple of weeks as well," Dylan added.

"I know, and I'm already exhausted." I chuckled.

"Tell me about it. Jackson barely sleeps."

"Oh please, you barely get up with him," Aurora added as we stopped outside of her office.

"Babe, I get up with him as much as I can. You know full well I need my rest," Dylan added, pulling her into his arms.

"So he says," Aurora added, smiling at me. "But between you and me, I can't even remember the last time he got up with him."

"I'd kill to have someone to fight with over who gets up with Mia." I chuckled.

"So, then, it doesn't end? These middle of the night moments?" Aurora asked, letting out a sigh, looking defeated.

I couldn't help but chuckle as Dylan let out a frustrated sigh.

"They do. Well, in some capacity. I will say they are easier now than they were. Having to guess what is wrong as they scream is hell."

"Well, I'm glad the two of you are talking about me as if I'm not even here,"

Dylan said, shaking his head and laughing.

"You are welcome, babe," Aurora added, pressing a kiss to his lips. "Good luck tonight."

"Thanks."

She then turned and pressed a kiss to my cheek,

wishing me good luck as well, and then made her way into her office while Dylan and I made our way to the locker room.

An hour later, we all sat listening as Coach Thompkins gave us our pre-game hype up before sending us to get ready. The moment he'd left the locker room I pulled my stuff from my locker and began getting ready. Knox sat across from me, buried in his phone.

I frowned as I watched him.

"What are you reading there?" I questioned. "You look deep in thought."

Knox looked up at me, a funny look coming over his face.

"What is it?" I asked again, this time concerned that perhaps he had gotten bad news.

"Have you checked Sports Hub?" Knox questioned, looking over at me?

"Nah, I haven't read that one in a while," I said, reaching for my jersey.

"Why what are you reading?" Colton asked, pulling his stuff from his locker, leaving it in a pile on the floor.

Dylan, Lucas, and Clay looked over at me. I could tell from the looks on their faces that they'd read the article Knox was reading, but I found it odd they had said nothing to me about it. Especially if Knox was bringing it to my attention.

"I think you should look," he said, leaning forward and passing me his phone which Dylan ripped from his hands.

"You know, I don't think it's worth reading right now. We have to get ready."

While I was curious about what he'd read, when I glanced at the clock, I realized Dylan was right. There was no way we had time to mess around.

IT WAS the start of the third period. We'd just returned to the ice, skating around to warm ourselves up. I was on my second lap of the rink when, out of the corner of my eye, I saw Scarlett behind the bench with one of the players from the other team.

She stood there, her hair pulled up the same way she'd always worn it. She was wearing the sweater I'd gotten her when I'd been away, shortly before we'd broken up. I was so trained on her, watching as she placed her hand on the other player's shoulder as she laughed at something he'd said, that I almost didn't see a player from the other team come at me. I leaped out of the way to avoid a collision, and that was when they rang the buzzer to start the third period.

Once I was in position, I glanced over to where she'd been, wanting to catch another look, only to find she wasn't there.

I looked behind the bench of the opposing team, checking each seat to find she wasn't there either. I was so trained on finding her, I didn't see the other player coming at me, and the next thing I knew, I was down on the ice, staring at the ceiling, the wind completely knocked out of me.

I lay there, not moving, and then Dylan looked down at me, then Brad from the medical team arrived.

"Are you okay?" Brad questioned. "You hurt?" he asked, placing his hand on the back of my neck, concerned that I'd injured myself when I hit the ice.

"Just had the wind knocked out of me. I'm good," I added.

The crowd cheered as I got up off the ice and made my way over to the bench with Brad, sitting out the next play. My eyes scanned the arena from where I sat, still looking for any signs of Scarlett, but seeing none.

WE ALL STOOD in the locker room, everyone quiet after the game we'd just lost. I was exhausted and had a bit of a headache, so I got changed and was just about ready to leave to head home and crawl into bed when Knox stopped me.

"What the hell happened tonight?" he asked. "That hit. We were worried that maybe you'd not be playing the rest of the game when you didn't get up right away."

I'd done everything I could to get Scarlett out of my mind, but nothing had worked. For weeks I'd done nothing but think of her, often messaging her brother to ask how she was doing but then chickening out. Instead, I would just have a conversation with him over nothing. Tonight, had been odd though, panic and excitement filling me when I was certain I'd seen her in the crowd.

"Yeah, it was like he came out of nowhere," I admitted.

"He was coming right for you. What do you mean, out of nowhere?"

"Exactly what I said."

"Didn't you see him coming at you?" Knox questioned.

I hadn't seen him coming, but that was because I hadn't been paying attention to the game.

"Look, I hate to admit it, but I thought I saw Scarlett in the crowd. It screwed me up."

Knox gave me a sympathetic look. While I'd convinced them all I was okay with the breakup, it had been a lie. Ever since I'd returned from my parents' after running into her I'd second-guessed myself, wondering if I should have given her a chance to explain things to me.

"Look, we know you've been having a hard time with this. We don't blame you, we know how much these women can fuck us up."

"Thanks, man."

"Remember earlier tonight when I wanted you to read that article?"

I nodded.

"I think you should read it."

I looked at him, alarm filling me.

"Is there something written about me?"

Knox nodded. "Before you fly off the handle, because I know you hate the media, it's not written about you in a bad way, but it is something I feel you need to read. The other guys think so as well, but they didn't feel it should be read before the game. In fact, Dylan gave me shit for trying to get you to read it."

"What the fuck does it say?" I questioned, now worried that it was something horrific like before.

"Just read it when you get home tonight, not

before," Knox said, placing his hand on my shoulder. "Trust me."

I'D DRIVEN HOME, quickly showered and crawled into bed, grabbing my phone and opening Sports Hub. I'd done what Knox had suggested, waiting until I'd gotten home. I navigated over to his message, clicking the link he'd sent me directing me to the article.

I stared at the title, swallowing hard.

Players Who Own Our Hearts written by Scarlett Green

Each one of us has a player that we long to watch long after the game is over. They are the ones that have us tuning in each game to see their next play and watching the after-game interviews to see what it is they are going to say. I've even spoken to fans who have learned to love the sport because of these players.

They are literally the magic behind the game, and if you are lucky enough to have one of them in your life, they are the magic behind that as well.

I first fell in love with the game as a young child. My brother played when he was younger, and me, being the youngest, was often forced to go with my parents to watch. At the time I hated the sport of hockey, but soon, I found myself lost in the sports world. A world I never left.

I was so close with my brother growing up, and I was often found attached to his hip. In fact, I often enjoyed hanging out with his friends more than my own.

That was where I met the man who owns my heart. I first met him at one of their college games, shortly after my brother got hurt, that injury ending his career. At first, I worried that I'd now be forced to end my love for the sport and this player since we wouldn't be at the games anymore. Only I soon learned that once you are in this hockey family, you stay there. He stayed, staying close to my brother and our family, eventually becoming one of my very best friends.

The one thing that taught me was that not only are these players the magic behind the team, but they are loyal to the ones who welcome them into their lives. It is probably my most favorite quality about them, that and the fact that you can rely on them whenever you need them.

Unfortunately, over the past few years, I've learned a hard lesson. That while these players are loyal and reliable, once you hurt them, you are no longer part of their circle. Being shut out is the most devastating feeling in the world.

The past six months have been the hardest six months of my life. I've moved from New York to Vancouver to take another new job, and then back to New York, taking another new job, and I've lost, for the last time, the one person who meant the world to me. Levi Anderson was that person.

See, I'd been coerced into writing an article and reporting on him by my boss at the last publication I'd worked for. She wanted one type of article, and while I knew that this would harm him, I quietly refused, turning in an article that was the opposite of what she wanted. I figured I'd done the right thing, that he'd be proud of what I'd written, only the joke was on me. What I should have done was stand up to her and refuse. Instead, she went behind my back sneaking into my own private files from interviews she booked for me using my name, rewrote the article, then published all the dirt under my name.

I can still remember the look on his face when he read it, the look he held when he told me never to talk to him again. I soon realized that my love for the game diminished, because I no longer could hold or feel that magic. He was gone, and there was nothing I could do about it.

I'm hoping to find that magic again, hoping to see his face once again look at me with the same smile and love that he once did. Whether it happens or it doesn't isn't for me to decide, so with that I sign off, encourage you to find the magic, and if you are lucky enough to have one of them in your life, then make sure you hold on to it because once the magic is gone, the world just doesn't seem to shine as bright as it once did.

I STARED AT MY SCREEN, noticing the words blurring. I put the phone down and wiped my eyes, immediately wanting to message her. Instead, I got up from the bed, making my way to the kitchen to get a drink of water to stop the ache that was there when my phone pinged.

DYLAN: Are you doing, okay?

I LOOKED AT MY PHONE, how the hell did they always know to message.

KNOX: Yeah, I finally let Lorelai read the article. She's in tears, she really laid it out on the line.

CLAY: WOW, that is all Peyton, and I have to say.

LUCAS: Ella is crying too. She wants to know if you're going to forgive her?

LEVI: I know, I'm at a loss for words. I think she owns my heart guys, no matter what everyone thinks.

COLTON: Fuck me, even I shed a tear.

DYLAN: Levi, you better take her back, she made the big guy shed tears.

CLAY: Didn't think that was possible.

LUCAS: That's funny.

LEVI: He does have a soft side, none of you guys have found it yet.

KNOX: Your woman did. So, what the hell are you waiting for? You going to go and get her?

LEVI: Thought everyone hated her?

DYLAN: The girls had a feeling something was wrong, they didn't hate her, they just felt something wasn't right. Of course we don't hate her, we barely know her.

CLAY: Yeah, what the hell are you waiting for? Go get her.

COLTON: If you don't go get her, I'll take her. Anyone who writes an apology to the entire world is one you need to be willing to put your heart on the line for, now go get her.

LEVI: Thanks, guys, for always being here.

I SHUT MY PHONE OFF, then stood in the kitchen, drinking down the first glass, refilling it before heading back to my room. I needed to come up with a plan, and then I'd head to her hotel in the morning. I was just about to go to my bedroom when I heard a tiny knock at my door. Glancing at the clock, I frowned. It was well past midnight.

I placed my glass on the counter and made my way over to the door and, without checking to see who it was, I pulled the door open, shock filling me when I saw who was standing there.

Chapter 19

Scarlett

I stood in the hall, my heart beating so hard I could barely breathe. They published the article over twenty-four hours ago. I had hoped to see Levi at the game, but somehow, he'd slipped out before I'd been able to speak with him. I'd been looking at my phone all night, praying for a message from him the entire day, to at least know he'd read what I'd written, but by the time I got back to the hotel tonight and still had heard nothing an hour later, I couldn't sit there any longer.

I was supposed to fly back to New York the day after next, and while it was still a while away, I didn't want to waste my time waiting. So, I got dressed, called a cab, and had them drop me at the building. Lucky for me there was someone who'd just left the building, so before the door locked, I'd snuck in and made my way to the floor Levi lived on. Now I stood, staring at his closed door, just having lightly knocked.

The last thing I wanted to do was wake Mia, so I stood there waiting to see if he opened the door before I knocked harder. Just as I was about to knock again, I heard the lock click and the door opened, my eyes falling on Levi.

We stood there looking at one another.

"Hi," I said, my voice barely audible.

I stood there, my heart aching as I stared at the man I'd fallen in love with, hoping and praying that he'd read the article and would find it in his heart to forgive me. I'd gone over this moment in my head what felt like thousands of times. I imagined he'd take one look at me and, without a moment's hesitation, pull me against him, kissing me, begging me never to leave his side again. Only it was far from what I'd imagined.

Instead, he stood there, staring back at me.

"Hey," he whispered.

"Could I come in?" I questioned, trying to read the look in his eyes.

Finally, Levi stepped to the side, not saying a word, but giving me enough space to let me into his place. He quietly shut the door and stepped away, placing his hands on his hips while he watched me. A funny feeling came over me as I stood in the entry of his place. I'd hoped he was going to make this easy on me, because I'd figured he'd have read the article.

"Levi, I know it's late, and I am so sorry to drop in like this, but I couldn't wait any longer."

I shoved my hands into the pockets of my jeans, then removed them, shifting from one foot to the other and back again, trying to find a comfortable position.

"It is late," he said, crossing his arms in front of his chest.

I knew that position well. Closed-off Levi, which meant he'd probably not read my article, and that he'd meant what he said the last time I saw him.

I shifted from foot to foot again, my mind screaming to just stop making a fool of myself and back away from him before this blew up in my face again. It wasn't worth the heartache. I'd suffered enough, I thought to myself.

For the first time in my life, I knew I was right.

While my eyes ran over him, I noted his body language again, making sure I was seeing what was really in front of me, then decided that this was a battle I'd never win no matter what I did. We really were over. Instead of saying another word, I turned away from him and put my hand on the door handle.

"Scarlett…" I heard him say just as I was about to turn the door handle.

I didn't turn around, I already knew what he was going to say, and I knew I'd never be able to look at him as he confirmed it.

I waited a moment, and then I felt his hands on my arms, my body jolting with electricity as he touched me. Then, without warning, he carefully turned me around and took my lips with his, kissing me hard.

My body instantly melted against him as his tongue washed through my mouth, and I let out a tiny moan as he nibbled my bottom lip while pulling me closer. When he pulled away, I felt as if I were going to fall into a heap on the floor, but he didn't let me go. Instead, he leaned forward, locking the door again, and took me in his arms and led me down the hall to his bedroom.

I LAY IN HIS ARMS, breathless and exhausted, wrapped in blankets. I opened my eyes and looked at the clock. It was almost ten. My body ached yet felt so relaxed, and I could feel the gentle puff of Levi's breath against the back of my neck as he slept behind me.

I shifted, gently stretching, trying not to wake him up, but the moment I stopped moving, he wrapped his arms around me tight, pulling me back against him.

"Were you trying to get away from me?" he murmured, pressing a kiss to my bare shoulder.

I couldn't help but let out a small giggle. "No way," I said, lacing my hand with his. "I never want to leave."

The moment he'd closed the door to his bedroom last night, he'd pushed me up against the door, kissing me hard as he worked quickly to undress me. Then he guided me over to the bed, where he kissed his way up my body, asking me for my forgiveness.

I had nothing to forgive him for, and I'd told him that, but he insisted he had to apologize for not allowing me to explain myself. Then, once he had me writhing on the mattress, he lay beside me, pulling me back against him, moving my leg to his hip and slid himself deep inside of me, slowly bringing me to climax repeatedly throughout the night, until we were both exhausted.

We continued laying there drifting in and out of sleep as we held one another. I felt the bed move and glanced over my shoulder to see Levi slip from the bed, his bare ass heading toward his ensuite.

I lay there, my body still exhausted and heard the shower start, then felt the bed sink.

"You coming to join me?" he asked, kissing my neck, before he left me again.

I finally kicked the covers off, making my way into the bathroom to see his silhouette in the frosted glass of the shower door.

I opened the door, stepping into the steamy shower, pulling the door closed behind me and placed my hands on his back.

"It's about time you got your ass in here," he said, turning and wrapping his arms around me as he pressed me up against the wall of the shower, lifting me up so I could wrap my legs around his waist.

"I know, I'm exhausted." I giggled as he kissed me.

"That's okay, give it a few minutes and you'll be even more tired than you are right now. Oh, and be as loud as you want, Mia's not home," Levi said as he sucked my nipple into his mouth and between his teeth.

I stopped him the moment he let my nipple go and placed both my hands on the side of his head.

"You mean to tell me I was quiet all last night for no reason."

Levi couldn't help but chuckle as he gave me the grin I loved the most.

"I'll make it up to you."

"How are you going to do that" I questioned, pretending to be annoyed.

"You'll see."

I lowered my hands from his face, and he spun me around, so I was facing the glass panel of the shower. He took my hands, placing each one up on the glass above my head, then took his foot and knocked on each of my ankles, signaling me to spread my legs, which I did. He gripped my hips, pulling me back, and slid himself deep inside of me.

"SO, YOU ARE OFF TO FLORIDA?" I questioned him as we stood in the airport.

Levi had decided that there was no need for me to stay at the hotel and that I'd just stay with him for the remainder of my stay in Vancouver, so I'd taken him up on that.

"Yeah, and then don't forget stopping in New York on my way home."

I nodded. I'd been hoping to have more time to rekindle than what we had, and while I tried not to allow my disappointment to show through, I knew it was.

"Listen, what is your schedule like?" Levi questioned, as we stood in line for me to get my boarding pass.

"Well, I have a full day of meetings for the rest of this week, and then I don't know."

"What would happen if you weren't there in person, but you were attending them virtually?"

"I have to do that sometimes, and it's never been an issue, but it's normally when I'm away on an assignment."

"Ah, I see. Well, what if I were your assignment?" Levi asked.

"How are you going to be my assignment? I don't think they will look at wanting to be with my boyfriend as a work-related assignment." I giggled.

Levi pulled me in closer, pressing a kiss to the side of my neck. "You don't?" he said, this time biting my earlobe sending a shiver of excitement through my body.

I closed my eyes, willing myself to fight the feelings that were running through me now, and shook my head.

"No, I don't."

I heard the announcement for my flight over the speaker and looked at Levi. I could already feel the sense of loss and we hadn't even said goodbye yet.

"I guess that means it time for you to go," he said, taking hold of both my hands in his.

"Unfortunately," I whispered, stepping closer to him, afraid to let him go.

"Message me when you get there okay."

"Of course."

Levi pulled me against him, kissing my mouth hard. I didn't want to leave him. Hell, after everything I never wanted to leave his side again. These months we'd been apart had almost killed me, and had he not taken me in that night I showed up at his door, I'd have fallen apart.

"I love you," he whispered the moment our lips parted.

"I love you too."

I turned around after I'd made it through the security and waved, then made my way to my plane.

Chapter 20

Levi - Three Weeks Later

"Alright, is that everything?" I asked Scarlett as she came walking out the door.

"I think so. Everything I had before is still in storage in Vancouver. I was planning on saving up and having it all trucked here," she said, wheeling a suitcase behind her while I carried the other one.

I opened the trunk of my rental and shoved her first bag in and then the second before turning to see her parents standing behind us on the sidewalk.

"You're certain this is what you want?" her mother said to her as she turned to face them.

"Yes, Mom, this is what I want," she whispered, giving her mother a hug.

The past three weeks had been hell for the pair of us. We'd taken so long to finally get together that neither of us wanted to waste another moment apart. While I'd been busy with the playoffs, Scarlett had been back here, and the time apart had nearly killed us.

Scarlett and I talked a lot during my time on the road, and once I had my flight booked to New York to pick Mia up, I'd called Scarlett and laid everything on the line. I didn't want to waste any more time. The moment she got on the phone, I jumped right to the point for my call, inviting her to move in with me. Unlike last time, waiting until everything was lined up wasn't going to work this time so, I told her on the same call that I wanted to marry her. I could still hear her cries as she sobbed on the other end of the phone while saying yes over and over. While it hadn't been the romantic proposal I'd wanted to give her, it was still part of our story.

"I'll miss my little girl," her mom cried as she pulled her in for another hug again.

"Sir," I said, holding my hand out for her father to shake.

"Look after my little girl."

"You know it," I said, placing my arm around Scarlett. "We need to get going, love. My parents are waiting for me to grab Mia so they can hit their afternoon card game," I said, watching her eyes filled with tears at the fact she was leaving home once again.

Scarlett hugged her mother, then her father, promising to come back home and visit soon. I smiled as she came over to me and wrapped her arm around my waist.

"Better yet, once we get Scarlett settled in, I'll fly both of you out for a week's visit," I added, shaking hands with her father, then hugging her mother. "That way you can meet Mia."

"We look forward to it, Levi."

I led Scarlett to the front of the car, opening the door and waiting for her to climb in before shutting it. Minutes later, we were on our way to my parents to get Mia.

When we pulled up, I put the car in park and cut the engine.

"So, let's surprise her," I said, looking over at Scarlett, who'd just finished wiping the last of her goodbye tears.

It was one of the characters of Scarlett I loved the most. She cried each time she left home, and even though she knew she'd be seeing her parents sooner rather than later, and she loved living on her own, she still was an emotional wreck each time.

"Really, you want to surprise her?" Scarlett asked.

"Sure do. You stay here. I'll be back with her. She'll

be ecstatic to see you," I said, taking hold of her hand and kissing the back of it before I climbed out of the car.

Moments later, I took hold of Mia's hand and kissed my parents goodbye, taking hold of her bag and picking her up. "Ready to head home?" I asked.

"Sure am. I forgot Potato." She pouted.

"How did you forget Potato?" I questioned.

Mia shrugged her shoulders.

"Did you have a good time with Grandma and Grandpa?" I questioned.

"Yeah, they took me to the zoo and to the reptile house, and now I want a lizard," Mia said, her eyes lighting up with excitement.

I couldn't help but chuckle. "I don't think Mrs. Fletcher will want to help with a lizard. Do you?"

"She will. I even have a name picked out."

"You do?" I asked.

"Yep, Marty. Mrs. Fletcher will love Marty," she said, wrapping her arms around my neck. "Please, Daddy."

I looked at my parents and shook my head as I walked out the front door. "We will see about Marty. Maybe Grandma and Grandpa will like to help with Marty."

"Not a chance." My mother laughed, grabbing

Mia and kissing her one more time before they headed off to their Bridge game.

As Mia and I headed to the car, Mia got quiet and rested her head on my shoulder.

"Everything okay there, sweets?" I asked.

"I miss Scarlett," she whispered.

Shocked, Mia hadn't mentioned Scarlett in a couple of months, but I was glad that she was waiting in the car. As we approached the car I saw the front passenger-side door open just as we'd planned, and out stepped Scarlett. Mia hadn't taken notice yet as she still rested her head on my shoulder, looking behind me. Scarlett stood there, smiling, waiting for Mia to take notice of her.

When I got to the car, I opened the trunk and then stepped to the side and gave Mia a little squeeze. She smiled at me and then noticed Scarlett, her eyes widening while an enormous smile grew on her lips.

"Scarlett!" she shouted.

"Hey, sweetie," Scarlett said, coming over and taking Mia from me, while I loaded the bag into the car.

"I can't believe you're here!" she said, pressing her lips to her cheek. "Are you staying?"

I looked over at Scarlett, who gave me a soft but sexy smile and then nodded. "If you'll have me."

"Daddy, did you hear that?" Mia said, getting excited.

"I did," I whispered, making my way over to the both of them, wrapping my arms around them.

"How about we head on home."

"Love to," Scarlett whispered.

We hopped in the car and headed off to the airport, on our way back to Vancouver where we were already starting to plan our life together.

Epilogue

Levi

"Okay guys, I'm gonna take off." I said, digging my keys out of my pocket.

We'd won our third game out of seven in the second round of the playoffs tonight and we'd all come to Illusions to celebrate.

"Are you able to drive the big guy home?" Knox questioned, glancing over to the corner where Lorelai was talking with Colton, trying to convince him not to drive.

I glanced at my watch. "I told Scarlett I'd be home

an hour ago, I'm already going to be in shit." I chuckled.

Lorelai came over to us, placing her hand on Knox's shoulder. "I'm going to take him home."

"What?"

"He said he'd go if I took him. So, take Dylan and Aurora home in your car, I'll take mine and drop him off, then I'll meet you at home."

I could tell from the look on Knox's face that he really didn't like that plan. "I'll go with you. Dylan and Aurora can just take my car."

"What about tomorrow? You have to pick up your mom from the airport, and I have to be at work early."

"Easy, Aurora can pick you up."

"She doesn't work in the morning, and it will be too early for you to drop me off at work. It's fine. I'll be fine, he's tired and drunk and just wants his bed." She said, leaning in and kissing Knox.

Knox looked at me as Lorelai walked over and took ahold of Colton's arm and leading him out of the room, waving goodnight.

"Alright, well, now that that is all figured out, I'm outta here."

WE LAY IN BED, wrapped in one another's arms, listening to the steady tap of rain against the windows. I pressed a kiss to Scarlett's bare shoulder hearing my phone vibrate against the nightstand for the fourth time.

"Levi, aren't you going to get your phone?" she murmured, placing her hand on mine.

"No, whatever it is can wait." I answered, running my hand down between her legs, as my phone went off again.

She let out a small giggle, rolling to her back and spreading her legs for me. "Is this all you ever think about?" She asked, closing her eyes, biting her bottom lip.

"Lately, yes." I whispered, pressing my lips against hers.

I reached over to the nightstand, opened the drawer and pulled out a condom as she reached down and took hold of my cock in her hand, gently stroking me.

"I'm starting to wonder if that is all you think about as well." I whispered, ripping the wrapper open and sliding it over myself.

I'd just gotten between her legs when my phone let out a shrill ring, causing us both to jump.

"For the love of.... this better be important." I

barked a little too loud, reaching over grabbing my phone.

I stared down at my screen seeing Dylan's name there. I let out a sigh, rolling off Scarlett in time to hear Mia start calling for me. I looked over at Scarlett with an annoyed look.

"I'll get her. You get that." Scarlett said, irritation lining her voice as she slipped from the bed throwing my robe on before making her way to Mia's room.

I let out a sigh as I answered the phone. "This better be important. I was just about to get some."

"Levi, are you able to come down here?" He questioned, completely ignoring what I'd said.

I frowned; I could hear it in his voice that something was wrong. "Everything alright?" I questioned.

"Yeah, just, can you get down here?" He repeated.

It was then I heard Knox mutter something in the background and Lorelai start to cry.

"Where are you guys?" I asked.

"Colton's… yes, I'm talking to him now. Just give me a minute. Levi, can you get down here?"

I quickly removed the condom off I'd just put on, then slid into my boxers and jeans. Something was wrong and whatever it was wasn't good. "I'll be there in twenty."

"See you then."

I got up and threw a shirt on over my head, just as Scarlett appeared carrying Mia in her arms.

"Going somewhere?" She questioned, looking at me with concern.

"Yeah, that was Dylan. Something's wrong, they need me to head over to Colton's." I said, grabbing my keys and wallet off the dresser.

"Will you be gone long?"

"Hopefully not, I'll message you once I find out what is going on." I said, pressing a kiss to her lips, then kissing Mia on the cheek.

"Okay, we'll be waiting." Scarlett said, laying Mia down on the bed then quickly slipping into the t-shirt and shorts she normally slept in before crawling into bed with Mia.

I PULLED up outside of Colton's house just as two police cars pulled away. The guys all stood in a group while Lorelai sat off to the side. I cut the engine and climbed out of the car and made my way over to where they all stood, immediately noticing someone was missing.

"What the hell is going on?" I questioned, walking over to them.

"It's bad." Clay answered.

Dylan was off to the side, on the phone, Knox beside him, his arm around Lorelai as she rested her head against his chest. I looked at them then at Clay, Lucas, realizing Colton who was missing.

"Where's the big guy?" I questioned.

It was then that Dylan and Knox came over and joined us. "Bout time you got here." Dylan said, shoving his phone in his back pocket.

"Yeah, well, things were happening. Now would someone tell me what the hell is going on."

"Colton's been arrested."

I looked at each one of the guys, shock surely written all over my face.

"Before you ask, we've already made all the calls that need to be made. It's not looking good." Dylan said, crossing his arms in front of him.

Colton had a reputation, but things had calmed since he'd come to the Dominators. He'd stayed out of trouble and out of the papers, until tonight.

"Pamela was calling Thompkins, who will surely be letting Larson know."

"Suspension?" Knox questioned.

"Probably," Dylan said, looking at me. "Has he mentioned anything to you about anything?"

I shook my head, "Not a word."

My cell phone let out a shrill ring and I pulled it from my back pocket to see Scarlett's name on the screen. No doubt she was worried. I stepped away, answering it.

"Everything okay?" she asked.

"It's not good babe. Colton has been arrested; we're going to be a bit. Is everything okay?"

"Yeah, was just worried. Guess I'll see you in the morning."

"I'll be home as soon as I can be."

I shoved my phone back into my pocket and made my way over to the guys just as Dylan was getting off his phone again.

"Thompkins and Larson want us all at the arena in twenty."

"Can you take me home first." Lorelai asked, still resting her head on Knox's chest.

"They want you there as well." Dylan said, looking at Knox. "She was here when it all went down."

AFTER A GRUELLING two-hour meeting with Larson and Thompkins, I finally walked through the door of our condo exhausted. After they'd spoken to Lorelai in private, they'd let us know that Colton was on suspension moving forward, and that they were working on getting a lawyer over to the police department to get him out of there. They'd forbid us to speak with the media until further notice.

I kicked my shoes off and made my way down the hall to see Scarlett and Mia sleeping soundly in the centre of the bed. The small bedside lamp was on, casting a small glow over them.

As I stood there, watching them sleep, suddenly I felt bad for Colton. He really was alone, and no matter how much we included him, not having a significant other in his life obviously affected him. It affected all of us, prior to the girls coming into our lives.

Scarlett stirred, opening her eyes a little, then took notice of me standing in the door to our bedroom. She propped herself up on her elbow, careful not to disturb Mia and looked at me.

"Is everything okay?" She asked quietly.

While I wanted to tell her everything that I knew from tonight, I knew now wasn't the time. I just wanted to crawl into bed and hold her in my arms.

"Eveything is good." I whispered, walking over and gently sitting on the edge of the bed, once again removing my clothes.

I slipped under the covers, reached up and shut the

light off, rolling onto my side and moving up against Scarlett. Tonight, if anything had made me realize just how lucky I was to have them both and as I closed my eyes and drifted off to sleep I hoped the Colton would eventually find someone like Scarlett, and that he'd get things in order once and for all.

GET A FREE BOOK

Sign up for my newsletter and I'll send you a free book.

https://geni.us/NLSignupBackMatter

What is coming next from S.L. Sterling

To see what is coming next from me visit my website
where you can always see the list of upcoming titles
that are currently available for preorder.

https://geni.us/ComingSoonfromSterling

About the Author

USA Today Bestselling Author S.L. Sterling was born and raised in southern Ontario. She now lives in Northern Ontario Canada and is married to her best friend and soul mate and their two dogs.

An avid reader all her life, S.L. Sterling dreamt of becoming an author. She decided to give writing a try after one of her favorite authors launched a course on how to write your novel. This course gave her the push she needed to put pen to paper and her debut novel "It Was Always You" was born.

When S.L. Sterling isn't writing or plotting her next novel she can be found curled up with a cup of coffee, blanket and the newest romance novel from one of her favorite authors.

In her spare time, she enjoys camping, hiking, sunny destinations, spending quality time with family and friends and of course reading.

To be notified of new releases or sales, join S.L. Sterling's private Mailing List. https://geni.us/NLSignupBackMatter

Get even more of the inside scoop when you join S.L. Sterling's private Facebook group, Sterling's Silver Sapphires: https://geni.us/SapphiresReaderGroup

His to Hold

Finding Forever with You

Vegas MMA

Dagger

Doctors of Eastport

Doctor Desire

Doctor Right

Doctor Frost

All I Want for Christmas (Contemporary Romance Holiday Collection)

Willow Valley

Memories of the Past

The Holiday Dilemma

Letters from the Heart

My Darling Christmas

Scars on my Heart

The Happy Holidates Series

Pop Tarts and Mistletoe

Champagne and Fireworks

Summer Nights and Fireflies